T
at To
and O
MU

"Like Conan Doyle's London, the Lockridges' New York has a lasting magic. There are taxis waiting at every corner, special little French restaurants, and perfect martinis. Even murder sparkles with big city sophistication. For everyone who remembers New York in the Forties and for everyone who wishes he did."

—Emma Lathen

"The versatility of Frances and Richard Lockridge knows almost no bounds."

—*New York Times*

"This husband and wife team is unexcelled in the field of mystery writing when it comes to a completely entertaining crime story."

—*St. Louis Post-Dispatch*

Pam and Jerry North made their first appearance in *The New Yorker* in the 1930s. In 1940, Richard Lockridge's first book-length mystery, *The Norths Meet Murder,* was published. Richard and Frances Lockridge went on to write dozens of Mr. and Mrs. North books, as well as numerous other mysteries. The Norths became the stars of a Broadway play and a movie as well as a long-running radio program and popular television series.

Books by Richard and Frances Lockridge

Death of an Angel
Death Takes a Bow
The Judge Is Reversed
Murder by the Book
Murder Comes First
Murder Has Its Points
Murder in a Hurry
Murder Is Served
Murder Within Murder
Voyage Into Violence

Published by POCKET BOOKS

MURDER HAS ITS POINTS

RICHARD AND FRANCES LOCKRIDGE

PUBLISHED BY POCKET BOOKS NEW YORK

POCKET BOOKS, a division of Simon & Schuster, Inc.
1230 Avenue of the Americas, New York, N.Y. 10020

ISBN: 0-671-47331-X

First Pocket Books printing April, 1984

10 9 8 7 6 5 4 3 2 1

POCKET and colophon are registered trademarks
of Simon & Schuster, Inc.

Printed in the U.S.A.

MURDER
HAS ITS
POINTS

1

When Gardner Willings came into a room he came in largely. The size of the room mattered very little, nor did the density of its population. The Gold Room of the Hotel Dumont was reasonably large, and on this November afternoon it was filled with the thirsty. And, Pam North thought, the talkative. And why Gardner Willings?

Strait, this afternoon, was the gate into the Gold Room and, at it, behind a table, Miss Arby from the office sat guard. On the table, it was to be assumed, invited guests dropped their invitations and received, in exchange, smiles. It did not seem to Pam, as she looked between people and around people, that Gardner Willings had hesitated long enough to drop. Which was, she supposed, like Gardner Willings. He was his own ticket of admission to anything. At least, he wasn't wearing a sweater. A slight ripple occurred in the crowd as Gardner Willings, his red beard a plow, proceeded through it toward the bar.

"I'm so sorry," Pamela North said. "It's so hard to hear anything, isn't it?"

The woman was quite tall. She was not, Pam thought, with sympathy, quite sure about the pink chiffon dress. Presumably she has a name and, Pam thought, it's skipped off my mind like a skittering stone off water. Somebody's wife, doubtless. Pam was slightly embarrassed by the thought. So, she added, am I. She said again that she was sorry, and added "so" for good measure.

"At home so much of the time," Pink Chiffon said. "At least I'd think—not that Ned isn't a dear but all the same—"

Pam North's mind riffled itself hurriedly. The unexpected advent of Gardner Willings did not justify rudeness; not even if Willings, famously, brought rudeness with him. She must have been talking about something to Pink Chiffon. Something concerning Ned.

"Of course," Pink Chiffon said, "he isn't like yours." She looked down at Pam North rather, Pam thought, as one looks at the feeble-minded. "Ned, I mean," Pink Chiffon said. "What I mean is, he doesn't *write*."

Husbands, of course. Husbands who did not go to offices. Husbands who merely stayed at home and *wrote*. No—WROTE.

"Goodness," Pam said. "Neither does mine, Mrs. Um-m-er."

She was looked at blankly. At that, Pink Chiffon had, Pam thought in spite of herself, something of a head start.

Pink Chiffon said, "But—"

"Publishes," Pam said. "He's—he's North Books. I mean—*this* is North Books."

She started to gesture around the room. Her knuckles hit something hard, and with a ping. "I'm so sorry," she said, to the waiter, who said, "Not at all, miss," in a hopeless voice.

"I was told," Pink Chiffon said, "that you were Mrs. Payne."

"I'm so sorry," Pam said, calling on her reserves of sorrow. "North. Mrs. Gerald." She laughed what she trusted was a hostess's laugh, and thought it sounded a little hysterical. I could have stayed at home, Pam North thought. I could go home. I'll tell Jerry I've got a—

"So hard to keep track of so many—" Pam said and, behind her, heard, "Pamela! *Darling!*"

She turned, too quickly, and the drink she held—had, it seemed to her, been holding for hours—sloshed. Thank heaven not on Pink Chiffon. She said, "Hello, Alice," to Alice Draycroft, and was conscious of inadequacy. "Darling," Pam added, and knew she missed the lilt. Alice did not fade; Alice kept the lilt. "Mrs. Um-mer—"

"Cook."

"Mrs. Cook. Miss Draycroft."

"Darling," Alice Draycroft said. "Such a *brawl*, isn't it?"

"Alice is an actress," Pam said. She felt she owed Mrs. Cook, née Pink Chiffon, that. At least that. Get her off on the right foot. Get myself off—

"You haven't a drink," Pam told Mrs. Cook, in a tone unexpectedly one of accusation. "I'll find a—"

An opening appeared and Pam took it. One learns self-preservation. One had better. "Over there," she told a waiter, in passing. "The one in pink. Talking to the one in gray, with mink."

She put her sloshed-out glass on a table, and took what might, with tolerance, be considered a martini from the waiter's tray. A tall, and very thin, and very dark-eyed youth in a white coat picked the used glass up and took it to a tray of other glasses, and lifted the tray to his shoulder. The shoulder of the white coat was dark from other trays. As he went off with it, he seemed to limp slightly.

Poor child, Pam thought. Everybody so gay and he carrying trays of dirty glasses—trays too heavy, filled with glasses marked by the lipstick of the gay. I'm getting maudlin, Pam thought. My soap-opera's showing. When Jerry was his age, Jerry was waiting table at college. *And* washing dishes. Where on earth is Jerry? I'll tell him I've got a—

"Pam," Tom Hathaway said. "Don't know if you've met Jim Self. Jim, this is Mrs. North. The boss's wife."

Self said, "Mrs. North." Pam said, "I'm so glad." Tom Hathaway—publicity, North Books, Inc.—said, "Get anybody a refill?" He looked quickly at Pam's glass, at the almost full glass of Jim Self. "Get myself one, then," Tom Hathaway said, and slipped from there. (One learns self-preservation. One had better.)

Mr. Self was not news media. A publicity man does not slip from news media, in whatever form. He might be connected, somehow, with the play. An actor? Or—

"I work in a bookstore," James Self said. "Why does your husband publish Anthony Payne?"

The direct type. One meets all types.

"Because he sells," Pam said. If he wanted it that way. "Why do you work in a bookstore?"

"I've heard of you," James Self said. "You're a murder fan."

Which was unfair—which was entirely unfair. When she got hold of Tom Hathaway—

The cocktail party, in dual celebration of the publication of Anthony Payne's *The Liberated* (North Books, Inc. $4.95) and the impending première of

Uprising, a play in three acts by Lars Simon, based on the novel by Anthony Payne, had been going on for almost two hours. As became the co-host, Jerry had arrived early. As became Jerry's wife, Pam had come with him. She had had a drink and a half, counting the sloshed, and neither had been cold and both had had too much vermouth. She had met what she counted, mentally, as hundreds of people and names had poured unregarded, unretained, through her mind. She had been bumped into, and had bumped. Her feet had been stepped on, and had stepped on other feet.

She had said, "I really don't know, I hardly know them," to a (presumptive) gossip columnist who had asked her what there was to the story that the Paynes were splitting up. She had said, "A good many people can't, of course," to woman (red wool suit, with slip showing) who had told her, with superiority, that she couldn't stand cats. She had been left to hold, and had left others holding. She had been photographed, with Jerry and Anthony and Lauren Payne, by a man who wanted just one more until her smile ached and had been told, reassuringly by Jerry, that the chances were a thousand to one nobody would ever publish the picture and that, anyway, she would look fine in it, and that she always did.

This was one of the few times she had met Payne. She had said, "Why?" with a gesture that amplified, and Jerry had said, "God knows. It seemed like a good—there's Mulloy of the *Times.* Better see that he's—" and vanished.

Mr. Self was quite probably right about the books of Mr. Anthony Payne. Mr. Self would no doubt prove right about many things. Men like Mr. Self quite often were. Mr. Self might well be—Mr. Self probably was—a dedicated seller of books, and of such there are too few.

"Murder," Pamela North said, "has its points. Excuse me, Mr. Self."

It was an exit line—not, clearly, one of the best, but one accepts what the harried mind provides. Pam North turned briskly from Mr. Self, this time not sloshing, and confronted hemming humanity, all of it, it suddenly seemed, very large. An exit line—and particularly one not really very good—requires graceful, if abrupt, departure. One should sweep away, head high. It occurred to Pam North that, if she were to leave Mr. Self, she would have to do it on hands and knees. She turned back, seeking escape beyond him. He was regarding her with an expression of acute detachment. She smiled weakly.

"Lots of people, aren't there?" Pam said, in a voice weaker than the smile.

"Payne's public," Self said. He spoke with bitterness.

"Just people," Pam said. "All kinds."

"Taken to make a world," Self said. "Ugh."

An angry young man? A little out of place? And not, really, quite that young.

"You came," Pam said.

"Yes," Self said. "Also—I go."

And went, parting the hemmers-in with right shoulder lowered. Pam followed into a semi-clearing. Self went on. Goodness, Pam thought. And he's not even a writer.

She looked around, seeking Jerry. The Gold Room of the Hotel Dumont was a large oblong. Jerry was not in sight. Nobody she knew was in sight. The bar ran the long way of the room. The crowd was thickest, there. There seemed, midway of the bar, to be a slight turmoil—a disturbed area. Gardner Willings, no doubt. That was what she wanted to see Jerry about, in addition to the report of an impending headache. Why—

Pam moved, partly by intention, partly as a result of pressure. Along the edges of the oblong there would be chairs and sofas. If she could not rest her ears—how could a hundred people, hardly more, make so great a din?—she might rest her feet. She worked toward the nearest edge. Let Jerry find her, for a change. Let—

It was easier as one retreated toward the nearest edge. There were sofas. The nearest—

"Phew," Pam North said, sitting on the half of a twin sofa now occupied by Lauren Payne. "In a word."

Lauren Payne, wife of the afternoon's lion, was slim and lovely; her hair was coppery and there seemed to be flecks of copper in her eyes. She turned to look at Pam and Pam was conscious, as she had been earlier, of a peculiar nervous anxiety in Lauren Payne's movements. In her movements—in her eyes? I'm imagining it, Pam thought, as she had thought earlier. I'm making it up as I go along.

"Oh," Lauren Payne said. Her voice was unexpectedly deep. She spoke, Pam thought, as if she had come back from some great distance. There was, for a moment, no recognition in the copper-flecked eyes. "Oh," Lauren Payne said again, "Mrs. North." Then she smiled; then she was back from wherever she had been. (From a place of creeping little fears? Nonsense. You're making it up as you go along, Pamela North.)

"It's nice to sit down," Lauren Payne said. "Very exciting and great fun but—it's nice to sit down." She smiled. No anxiety in her smile. "Such a lovely party," she said. "We're both so—happy about it."

She was animated, suddenly. She seemed, to Pam North, to pull animation about her. A moment before—as Pam moved quickly toward the empty seat, only half conscious of its other occupant—Lauren had looked weary, drained. Pam remembered that now—now that animation became a cloak, shiny as a cellophane wrapper. One saw something; afterward assessed the seen. Lauren Payne had looked drained.

"A lovely party," Lauren said again, and made her face sparkle with the loveliness of it all.

"I'm glad," Pam said, remembering she was, by association, hostess. "A little—noisy."

Lauren Payne did not deny that it was a little noisy. She said, "Who are they all? I mean—"

"I know," Pam said. "I often wonder. Bookstore people. Newspaper people and there's always a hope of reviewers, but most of them don't. And gossip columnists and people who write columns about books. And people who work for reprint houses and this time, of course, people connected with the play." Pam North searched her mind briefly. "And writers," she said.

As she spoke she had looked around the crowded room, seeking guidance. Now she looked back at Lauren Payne.

And the animation had been wiped away. Pam was not certain that attention had not been wiped away with it. Lauren turned toward her again, and again Pam was conscious of an abruptness in the movement of Lauren Payne's body—a kind of jumpiness. It was as if—as if, somewhere, somebody had said, loudly, "Boo!"

"So good for Anthony," Lauren said, and pulled animation once more about her. "So—so stimulating. I—"

She stopped speaking and looked up at a man—a very tall and handsome man, dark-haired, mobile of face—who had suddenly appeared and stood in front

of them and looked down. Looked down, very specifi-
cally, at Lauren Payne; looked at her as if he were, in
some fashion, measuring her; in some fashion questioning her.

"Fine," she said. "Perfectly fine, Blaine." She
smiled up at him—smiled a smile of animation.

He looked at her with continued seriousness, still in
appraisal. He was, Pam thought, looking at her as a
doctor might at a patient, seeking in face and body,
listening for in voice, hints for diagnosis. I might as
well not be here, Pam thought. Here, I intrude. I might
much better not be here.

"You know Mrs. North, of course?" Lauren said.

The handsome dark man—he must be, Pam thought,
about Lauren's age; certainly far younger than Anthony Payne—looked at Pam as if, for the first time, he
realized two women were sitting on the sofa. For a
second the intenseness of his scrutiny did not alter.
Then he smiled. Smiles change all faces; his was more
changed than most. He said, "Mrs. North," and in a
tone of pleasure. One could not fault the tone. One
had, of course, no reason to believe in it. He did go to
the trouble. There was that.

"Blaine Smythe," Lauren said. "With 'y' and 'e.'"

"But Smith for all that," Smythe said. "The fault of
ancestors."

There was a little of England in his speech. It was
not emphasized.

"Very jolly party," he said. "Quite a thing for
Tony."

"I was just telling Mrs. North—" Lauren said, and
Pam, seeing a chance, stood up.

"And I," she said, "had better circulate in it. So
nice, Mr. Smythe. Mrs. Payne."

This time she could exit, although this time with no
line left behind. She looked back, before the crowd

15

surrounded her. Blaine Smythe had sat down beside Lauren. He was leaning toward her. He seemed to be talking very quickly. Pam had a feeling that he was talking firmly. Me and my feelings, Pam thought, and continued her search for Jerry.

She sighted him at some distance and, for a time, it was as if she had sighted a mirage. Progress toward him was difficult; one inched along an obstacle course. Item: A food columnist who was compiling a cookbook which Jerry hoped to publish. Cookbooks never fail. Would Pam tell Jerry what a wonderful party it had been, in spite of the (so understandable) dryness of the canapés? Item: Had Pam met Faith Constable, of whom, of course, she knew, as didn't everybody? Faith Constable—of whom Pam most certainly knew, as who did not?—was a quick, somehow shimmering, woman in (it had to be, but challenged belief) her middle fifties. She, further, had a starring—anyway, co-starring—role in the forthcoming production of Lars Simon's adaptation of *Uprising*. She was also, although now Mrs. Constable, the first wife of Anthony Payne.

Faith was, admittedly, fun. The malicious often are. Did Pam know that Gardner Willings was there? With, Faith would suppose, blood in his eye. The eye, of course, dear Tony had blackened. "Tony's dear, dirty little mind," Faith said, fondly. Did Pam darling know—

Jerry wasn't where he had been. He had been talking to a man who, from that distance, appeared to be Livingston Birdwood (Productions) who was half-giver of the party. He and Jerry, Pam suspected, might be now, belatedly, asking each other why the hell? Now Birdwood—if it was Birdwood—was moving somberly toward the bar, and Jerry was not—

Yes, there he was. Talking to Tom Hathaway. Not

thirty people, not half a dozen obstacles, away. He
was even within smiling distance; he looked between
people, over people, saw Pam and smiled at her. The
smile was somewhat abstracted, but there. While he
smiled across at Pam, he listened to Tom Hathaway,
and now and again nodded his head. Hathaway
seemed to be talking earnestly. Pamela North pointed
herself and started. And, from a knot of people, a hand
reached out—like the tentacle of a mildly absent-
minded octopus—and took her arm. She looked. She
said, "Hello, Bertie. I'm trying—"

Albert Watson was art director of North Books, Inc.
He was white-haired and sixty, and entirely affable.
He said, "Man here says he hasn't met you. Told him
he should. Eh?"

"Of—" Pam said.

"Famous playwight," Watson said. It occurred to
Pam that Bertie had had several. Everybody but me's
had several, Pam thought. "Present Mr. Simon," Bertie said. "Lars Simon. Famous playwright."

Pam said, "How d'ye do, Mr. Simon. I—"

"Making the play out of Tony Payne's book," Bertie
said. "Having his troubles, he says."

"Oh?"

Lars Simon was a slight, quick man. He had receding black hair. He put his right hand to his forehead
and pushed the heel of the hand back hard against his
head. Probably, Pam thought, he'd rubbed the hair off.

"God," Lars Simon said, simply. "You know
Payne, Mrs. North?"

"Not well," Pam said.

Lars Simon now put both hands to his head and
pushed. A wonder, Pam thought, he hadn't rubbed it
all off.

"Clutching at straws," Simon said. "No influence
with him then? Your husband?"

"None," Pam said. "I doubt whether Jerry—why, Mr. Simon?"

"Too long," Simon said, and looked at Pam with what appeared to be desperation in his dark eyes. "Take me all night. If you—say—told Payne to drop dead it wouldn't do any good?"

"No."

"To take a trip around the world?"

He smiled, now. The smile was somewhat bitter, but it was a smile of sorts. Pam smiled back, assuming banter somehow intended. She shook her head.

"Atlantic City? For"—he looked momentarily at the ceiling and seemed to count on his fingers—"four weeks and three days? Until we open?"

Pam shook her head again. She smiled again. She thought, Jerry will get away again.

Lars Simon sighed heavily. It was a sigh planned for notice.

"Mrs. North," Lars Simon said. "Promise me something. Never sign a collaboration agreement with a novelist. Not one that lets him sit in. Not one that gives him anything to say about—anything. Anything at all. Promise?"

"Absolutely," Pam said. "Faithfully."

"You have nice hair," Simon said. "Look at mine. Novelists. You do promise?"

"Never sign a collaboration agreement with a novelist," Pam said. "Cross my heart."

Presumably, Lars Simon also had had a few. Pam again felt herself deprived. Of course with people just met it is often hard to tell. This is, in Pam's not too limited experience, especially true with writers.

"My good deed for the day," Lars Simon said. "When you see your husband next, Mrs. North, tell him that I had a wonderful time at his wonderful party. If you see Mr. Payne—" He paused; he spread hands in a gesture of hopelessness. He said, "No. You're too little. And the wrong sex. And—" He shrugged. Unexpectedly, he thrust his hand forward and Pam took it. His was a wiry hand, alive in her own. He said, "Be of good cheer," and, abruptly, released her hand, turned, and went. Pam looked after him. She said, "Well."

"Interesting young man," Bertie Watson said. "Doesn't care too much for our Mr. Payne, apparently. Gets in his hair, would you say?"

"Precisely," Pam said. "Precisely what I'd say, Bertie." There were three other people standing in the small circle of which Lars Simon had, rather vividly, been a center. Pam had never seen any of them before, so far as she could recall. Neither, apparently, had Bertie Watson. Spectators, evidently. People who just happened to be there. Pam smiled at them, told Bertie that she would be seeing him, went in the direction opposite that taken by Lars Simon.

Jerry had disappeared again. Selfishly at the bar? While she—

No. In a corner. With the afternoon's lion. Also, she had begun to think, to several the afternoon's pain. Pam shuddered at her own pun and tried open-field running, although necessarily at a walk, toward her husband and the singularly maneless lion.

Anthony Payne was a big man and a solid one. He had a roseate face and a jutting chin. He was also, and completely, bald. For some reason Pam had not been able to pin down, this baldness gave him a formidable appearance. He looked, Pam had told Jerry after her first meeting with his valuable author, rather like a frontiersman who had lost a round to an Indian.

He was now jutting his chin at Jerry, who listened, smiled faintly, nodded his head from time to time. Jerry looked past him, saw Pam, and his expression told her to come right along. She tried to. She said,

19

"Sorry"—an afternoon for light sorrow—and "excuse me" and "if you don't mind, please" and advanced twenty feet and the channel closed.

What closed it was the thin back of the busboy in the white coat—the one for whom, earlier, Pam had felt sympathy until she thought of Jerry's onetime washing of dishes.

The boy—the extraordinarily thin boy—was standing rigidly, his gaze fixed on— Well, from the angle, on Gerald North, publisher, and Anthony Payne, author—author who had, as Pam had said of him, also after first meeting, taken Africa under his wing.

Pam cleared her throat, and the boy stood rigid, did not move. She said, "Please?" and said it gently. Said it, it became evident, too gently, since there was no response. She touched a thin arm under a white coat and the boy turned and, for an instant, glared down at her. Then the glare faded and he said, "Sorry, miss," and moved aside, holding a tray with two highball glasses on it.

Pam went through. The glare bothered. A—an expression of hate? But not for her. That was obvious. A—a leftover glare, lingering for an instant on a young face? He could hardly have been looking so at Jerry. He'd better not have been. If the thin young man thought he could—

Jerry reached for her arm and held it gently and said, "Hi. Having fun?"

"Hi," Pam said. "Hi, Mr. Payne. Jerry, did you know that Mr. Will—"

"Yes," Jerry said.

"Did you?"

"No. I didn't. I've just been telling Tony—"

"Gardner Willings," Payne said, "thinks he's God Almighty."

20

Payne had a high-pitched voice. It did not go with the chin.

"And," Payne said, "if he thinks, if anybody thinks, I won't say what I want to say about the overrated son of—" He left it there, presumably out of deference to Pam's sex. A curious and unexpected reticence, Pam thought. "We were talking about that review of mine," Payne said. "Hear Willings is telling people he's going to make me eat it. Like to see him—"

"Take it easy, Tony," Jerry said. "He's still at the bar, lapping. As for the review—nobody's arguing you shouldn't say what you want to say. Only—"

Pam had read the review. She had thought of it when she saw Gardner Willings so largely enter. It was why she had thought that, if Jerry didn't already know that Willings had arrived, invited or—more probably, now confirmedly—uninvited, Jerry had better be told.

The review, written by Payne, had appeared two Sundays before in the book review section of the *Globe-Express*. It had been of Willings's new book— *Ancient of Days,* about the slow (and to Pam not too interesting) death of an African tribal leader. And the review must have—Jerry had told her that the talk was it rather prodigiously had—given pause to the editors of the book review section.

The editors, like those of many review sections, thought it well to have novelists review the books of other, and if possible similar, novelists. This resulted, for the most part, in affable reviews, soothing alike to the reviewed, their publishers and potential readers. It proved novelists without jealousy of, or malice toward, their like. Pamela North summed it up perhaps more succinctly. The rule, she had once told Jerry, was simple: Never bite the hand that might bite back.

In his lengthy discussion of *Ancient of Days,* by

Gardner Willings ($4.95), Anthony Payne had, to put it gently, ignored this rule. He had begun softly enough, using the play-it-safe, or weasel, "perhaps." "In view of this new novel by the widely acclaimed Mr. Willings, it is perhaps time to do some admittedly agonizing reappraisal," Payne had begun. "It is not a pleasant task, but—"

Payne had gone on for some hundreds of words, and there had been nothing in any of them to indicate that he found his task unpleasant. He had mentioned the "now stale obviousness of the once acclaimed style." He had referred to Willings as a "self-elected authority on the dark continent." He had also called Willings "the synthetic he-man of American letters."

(The editors had hesitated long and thoughtfully over that one, but had let it stand.)

Reviews of fiction do not, of course, disturb many— they raise tempests in few and smallish teacups. But there had not been so many startled yaps from indignant readers emitted since John O'Hara, many years before, had compared Hemingway to Shakespeare, to the latter's disadvantage. And Willings, in New York for the publication—instead of in the Virgin Islands, where he had lived for years, and created many legends and more wisecracks—had told a good many people that he would make Payne eat not only the review, but the entire section in which it appeared—a section profitably heavy with advertising.

"After all," Payne said now, "he's a has-been who never was, and if he wants to make—"

It was after seven, and the party had thinned somewhat. High-pitched voices carry, particularly when they are used with emphasis.

There was a stirring at the bar, a ripple among the still-packed drinkers. There was, suddenly, comparative silence in the end of the room the Norths and

22

Payne stood in—a silence broken, with painful distinctness, by the tag-line of a story which, in more prudish days, would not have been told in mixed company. (Which, Pam thought, God knew this was.) After the tag-line, unfortunately spoken by a woman, had trilled out, the silence was momentarily almost complete.

It was broken by a wordless sound which might have been made by a large and very angry cat.

2

There was a convulsion at the bar, as if a very localized earthquake had occurred there. Men swayed outward from a center; a woman said, shrilly, "Ouch!" And a large, square man came from the eye of the disturbance—a man with a crisp red beard; a man wearing a light gray suit and a dark blue shirt. Folded newsprint bulged one of the pockets of the suit's jacket. Oh dear, Pam North thought, he's really going to.

Gardner Willings, advancing on his all-too-evident prey, did not adopt open-field running. Gardner Willings opened the field, as a plow a furrow. He leaned slightly forward as he walked, heavy shoulders set for impact. Pam looked at Anthony Payne. It occurred to her that Mr. Payne seemed to grow perceptibly less large. His chin no longer really jutted. If anything, it nestled. But, nevertheless, he stood and waited. Had he not—see *The Africa I Know,* by Anthony Payne (North Books, Inc. $3.95)—once stood firm against enraged tribesmen? Pam looked again at Gardner Willings. Better, she thought, enraged tribesmen.

Willings bowled aside a gossip columnist who had not been quite quick enough. Willings stopped, at the last possible moment, in front of Payne. He looked at Payne. He leaned even closer and looked at him from inches.

"Seem to have teeth," Willings said, loudly. He reached a large, red-haired hand out toward Payne as if to make sure. Payne drew his head back. He said, "See here, Willings," in a voice which seemed even more highly pitched than before.

"Cream and sugar?" Willings said. "Or mix it with pap. That's it—pap." He turned slightly and spoke loudly to nobody in particular. "Bring pap," he said. "Pap for Payne."

Nobody moved. One waiter shook slightly, as if about to move, but thought better of it.

"Listen, Mr. Willings—" Jerry said, still standing beside Payne. I wish Jerry'd move away, Pam thought. One of them might miss.

"You," Willings said. "Drop dead. Whoever you are. Or, you want to help him?"

He took the folded newsprint out of the bulging pocket. It was the *Globe-Express* literary supplement of two weeks before. There was no doubt of that. Folded lengthwise it a little resembled a club. Book advertising grows heavy in mid-November.

"Butter?" Willings said. "It'll run to butter. Don't want to make it hard for you, you pig-nit." (Pig-nit?) "Apple worm. Synthetic, huh? I'll synthetic you, you—you—" he looked at Payne as if he saw him for the first time. "Hairless toad."

He waved the still folded copy of the *Globe-Express* book review section back and forth in front of Payne's face. Then he thrust it toward Payne's mouth.

25

"Eat," he said. "For what you are about to receive, Payne in the anatomy, may the medicine men you never came within miles of make you—"

He did not finish. He lunged toward Payne with the folded paper. It was as he did this that it became apparent that he was very drunk. As he lunged he swayed.

And as he lunged, Payne hit him—hit him on the chin. It did not seem to those watching that the blow was a hard blow. But Gardner Willings reeled back and was on the floor before anybody could catch him.

He sat there for a moment and began to shout. He didn't bother to invent insults this time. He used those at hand—those always at hand. As he shouted at Payne, he started to get up.

The paralysis which seemed to have set in everywhere ended then. Several men grabbed Willings and helped him up, and held him. Jerry and, emerging suddenly, Tom Hathaway, held Payne although (Pam thought) needlessly. Payne, in fact, looked not only frightened but vastly surprised.

Willings stopped talking. He stopped a scarcely begun struggle to be free.

"All right," he said, in a quite ordered voice, "I won't hurt the two-bit phony."

He tossed the book section on the floor. He kicked it away with contempt. He looked again at Payne, and this time his gaze seemed very different. There was, this time, a coldness in his fixed stare at the hairless man. And then, for the first time, Gardner Willings became a formidable man, and a rather frightening one. Before, in a somewhat dreadful way, it had all been a little funny. Now—now there was nothing funny about the way Willings looked at Anthony Payne.

I wouldn't, Pam thought, want to be the man who

knocked Gardner Willings down, turned the tables on Willings, made Willings look—look like a clown. Because, Pam thought, in spite of everything—pose and bluster and everything—Gardner Willings is a dozen Anthony Paynes. I wouldn't want to be Payne against the other eleven.

Willings turned and walked away—walked very straight, very steadily, and people got out of his way. Willings walked out of the Gold Room and it was only after he was out of the room, out of sight, that the buzzing started. Even then it had an oddly artificial quality, like the ad-lib crowd-murmurs of a stage scene.

Pam had moved away from Jerry and from Payne, being allergic to falling gladiators, especially large ones. She moved back.

"Sorry," Jerry said to Payne. "Wouldn't have had this sort of thing happen." He looked around the room, which was suddenly much emptier than it had been only a minute or two before. Those associated with the press—gossip columnists of Broadway, commentators on the literary scene—were getting out of there. There was no doubt to what purpose. "God knows," Jerry said, and shuddered slightly. It is always to be hoped that literary cocktail parties will engender publicity but—

"Blustering bully," Payne said. Color had returned to his face. The jaw jutted again. "Time somebody stood up to him."

Gerald North looked at Payne. He looked at him as if Payne somewhat surprised him.

"Yes," Jerry said. "I suppose so, Tony. Only—"

Payne turned and waited. It seemed to Pam, watching, that his expression was truculent.

"Nothing," Jerry said. "Let's get ourselves a drink. Pam?"

27

"By all means," Pamela North said.

Business at the bar had noticeably slackened. It was possible to have drinks made to order, and to the Dumont's usual, and admirable, formula. It was even possible to find a table to sit at while drinking. Jerry had fallen silent; even when Hathaway and, later, Livingston Birdwood joined them, he continued to appear abstracted. Pam could guess why. He was reading headlines probably at the moment being written.

"Gardner Willings K. O.ed." That, or something like that, would be one of them. "Noted Writers in Party Brawl." "Book Review Leads to Fisticuffs." "Anthony Payne Invited to Eat Words; Declines with Fists."

Pam put a hand on Jerry's, under the table. "Read 'em and weep," Pam said, softly. Gerald North's response was brief. "God," Jerry said. He finished his drink and beckoned a waiter.

Payne, also, seemed abstracted, as if he were having second thoughts. As well he may, Pam thought. He seemed, further, to have developed a sudden and considerable thirst. Dutch courage? But Willings was, now, long gone.

And so, Pam thought, looking around the room, half listening to Hathaway's assurance that there was really no harm done, to Birdwood's skeptical "hm-mm," is almost everybody else. Only two waiters, now; several busboys now, and most of them by no means boys. The thin youngster whose face had momentarily showed hate—of whom?—was not in sight, although now was certainly a time for busboys. Lauren Payne was not in sight—no doubt she had developed the headache Pam had herself thought of acquiring. The man who had looked anxiously at her— oh yes, Blaine Smythe—he also was not to be seen. Nor Faith Constable; nor Alice Draycroft. Of course not Alice—Alice was working; long ago Alice must have gone for a quick, before-performance, dinner. Lars Simon had—at least she was sure he had—left before the brawl. Pity to miss the fireworks, which he probably would have enjoyed. (Even if, in the end, Anthony Payne had eaten nothing so indigestible as newsprint.) Everybody she had—no, there was Pink Chiffon. Pam hoped that the woman she was talking to was, this time, really the wife of an author. (One who could be compared to Ned.)

Jerry looked at his watch and shook his wrist and looked at it again.

"What say," Jerry said, "we get some dinner? Tony? Birdwood? Tom? Find Mrs. Payne and—"

Payne shook his head. His wife had "gone up." Headache. Probably taken something to put her to sleep. Subject to headaches, poor thing.

"Here?" Birdwood said, with doubt. He was younger than one would have thought, since he was "Productions, Inc." He was tall and rangy and had deep-set eyes.

Payne shook his head, violently.

"No," Jerry said. "Somewhere—quieter."

They went out of the Gold Room and through the lobby and stood on the sidewalk in front of the Dumont among others waving for taxis. They had, Pam thought, picked a bad time. All that remained of the party seemed to have joined them. They'd be hours getting a taxi. And they all needed food by now. Anthony Payne especially, Pam thought. Payne did not seem entirely steady on his feet. Jerry took his arm.

The Dumont's doorman stood, perilously, in the middle of the street and blew a shrill whistle furiously, and, as need arose, dodged expertly. Down the street a cab stopped; started up again, and its roof light went on. The doorman beeped at it almost hysterically; grabbed it as it approached. And the lead-off couple, looking smug to all who were still to wait, got in and were driven off. Jerry waved in the air and the doorman nodded his head, but then gestured at others who waited. It will be forever, Pam thought.

Their "party"—try to think of something else to call it—was a group of five, wedged some distance from the curb, with Payne swaying slightly in the center—swaying and, at intervals, turning from side to side. He was also talking. He was talking about Willings. He had now, it appeared, reached in his own mind a satisfactory explanation of Willings. Willings was crazy. He turned to Pam and said, "That's it. The poor old bastard's gone nuts." Pam said of course, and that that was probably it. "Crazy as a loon," Payne said, and turned to say it to Jerry, who held his arm. "Sure," Jerry said. "That's it." "Ought to be locked up in a loony bin," Payne told Tom Hathaway. "Right you are," Hathaway said. "Only explanation." "Been showing in his work for years," Payne said to Livingston Birdwood, who looked discomfitted and said, "Hm-mm."

"What I say—" Anthony Payne said, and dropped dead.

This was not, of course, instantly apparent. It was apparent that he dropped, and, falling, pulled his arm from Jerry's not insistent hold. He dropped to the sidewalk, in a huddle, twitched violently, and more or less straightened out and lay still.

"Poor bloke's passed—" Hathaway began, and did not finish. Jerry was sitting on his heels by Payne and looked up at Hathaway and shook his head, and then Hathaway squatted on the other side of Payne and looked and said, *"Good God!"* and then put his head back and began to look, apparently, up at the sky.

There was blood by that time. It came out of a small, neat hole almost in the middle of the top of Payne's bald head.

It was the doorman who ran, heavily, to call the police.

Every now and then in New York somebody comes into the possession of a rifle and goes either to a roof or to a high-up window and indulges in target practice, with people as targets. There is no rational explanation of this; many things happen in New York, and in other cities, which do not admit of rational explanation. The police of New York are, to this, resigned. "Town's full of crackpots," any policeman will tell anyone. There is nothing to do about crackpots except to try to catch them.

And this, of course, is made the more difficult by the fact that reason does not anywhere enter in. Premeditated crimes, including murder, are reasonably designed, and hence may be considered by the rational mind. In professional crime there is always the hope, usually justified, that a squeal will sound, particularly if pressure is properly applied in likely places, most of which the police know. Police laboratories sift the logic of fact and present the siftings for addition. ("The cord with which the woman was tied up is of a type used by upholsterers. This particular sample was manufactured by the Such and Such Company, which has sales outlets in—")

But none of these methods of operation is of much use when somebody has shot somebody else merely for the fun of it.

During the November on a late evening of which Anthony Payne had dropped dead on the sidewalk in front of the Dumont Hotel, there had been seven snipings in the five boroughs, four of them in Manhattan. Three of these had occurred earlier in the week Payne died in. One child had been slightly grazed; a young woman had been shot in the leg, again not seriously; an elderly man had been barely nicked, but he had died of a heart attack in the moment of his shocked surprise.

The Eighteenth Precinct, with a station house in West Fifty-fourth Street, had had its fill of snipings. Nobody had so far been caught and it did not seem likely that anybody would be. Such prankish marksmen are, in the ordinary run of things, caught either at once or not at all. (Somebody sees a rifle sticking from a window and then there is a place to start; a building to surround, to go over inch by inch.)

In none of that month's incidents had the police had luck. One man or woman, or boy or girl, might be responsible for Manhattan's four and, for that matter, for the one in the Bronx and the two in Brooklyn. This was not likely, nor, on the other hand, was it likely that the sudden sequence of such shootings was merely a matter of chance. Crackpots ape crackpots. "Might be fun to try that," one crackpot thinks, reading of another crackpot's exploit.

"Got another one," Detective Pearson said to Detective Foley in the squad room of the Eighteenth Precinct. "We're to get cracking, Joe. A D.O.A. this time."

"Nobody will have seen anything," Detective Foley said. "Also, everybody will have scrammed. If anybody heard anything, he thought it was a backfire."

"Yep," Detective Pearson said. "Let's get cracking, Joe."

"The homicide boys?"

"Probably not fancy enough for them," Detective Pearson said. "Just some poor bloke with a hole in his

32

head, on account of this prankster sees a likely head."

"Anybody we know?"

"Not a regular," Pearson said. "Just some poor Joe trying to get a taxi. In front of the Dumont."

"Some ways," Foley said, "this is a hell of a town."

Victim: Anthony Payne, white American; 57; 5 feet 11; 195 pounds; occupation, writer. House in Ridge-field, Connecticut; for some days staying at the Hotel Dumont. Married; wife in hotel room—fourth floor, front; under mild sedation when notified by friends. Further sedation considered necessary by house physician.

Nature of wound: Gunshot, probably .22 long rifle (autopsy to verify) in top of head. Apparent course of bullet, straight down. Unconscious almost instantly; dead in seconds; dead on the arrival of an ambulance; body removed to morgue.

"They don't grow wings," Pearson told Foley. "Nobody was hovering over his head."

"He leans a little this way," Foley pointed out. "Leans a little that way. All our joker has to do is wait until he leans where wanted."

Pamela North and Gerald North; Thomas Hatha-way and Livingston Birdwood had waited. They had been asked to wait, as those closest to Payne when he died. And Mrs. North had been the one who had gone up to the room in which Lauren Payne dozed, under the mild influence of a barbiturate, and wakened her to tell her that Anthony Payne was dead.

Pam had been a little surprised by the wide-eyed, protesting shock with which her news had been received. She did not know precisely why she had been surprised; she knew nothing of the relations between Lauren and her husband. Anthony might have been all her life to Lauren Payne. Why, then, be surprised at the near-hysteria that followed shock, at the need for sedation so quickly recognized by the house physician?

They had waited in the lounge of the Dumont, with Birdwood looking often at his watch. When they arrived, Foley and Pearson looked very much like policemen in plain clothes. Pearson said it looked like being one of those things—one of those things with no sense to it.

"Might have been anybody," Foley said. "Any one of you. Got hit, I mean."

Pam had already thought of that, shivered at the thought of that. It might most easily have been Jerry, who had been standing closest—who had had a hand on Payne's left arm, to steady him.

"About all we can do," Pearson said, "is to try to work out where the shot came from. See what I mean? It went straight in, looks like. As if whoever fired was shooting straight down. But it couldn't have been, because what's directly above him? Air."

"He was—swaying a little," Pam said. "He was—" She stopped.

"Payne had had several drinks," Jerry said. "I suppose we all had. We'd been at a cocktail party, you see. Payne showed his, when he got out in the air especially. So—"

"Sure," Foley said. "He swayed a little, leaned this way a little and that way a little. Which way was he leaning when it hit him?"

Jerry shook his head slowly and looked at Pam, and she shook hers. "I haven't the faintest idea," Tom Hathaway said. "I wasn't looking at him," Birdwood said. "I was watching the doorman trying to get a cab."

"If it was toward this hotel," Pearson said, "then the shot probably came from here. Or the place next

34

door. If he was leaning toward the street, then our man could have been in the hotel across it—the—" He looked at Foley.

"King Arthur," Foley said. "Or the hotel up the street from it. Or the roof of the parking garage."

"It's about all we've got to go on," Pearson said. "It's not much, is it?"

"Things like this, we never get much," Foley said. "That's the size of it. Nobody noticed which way he was leaning? Which way he was facing?"

Still nobody had.

"I don't suppose," Pearson said, "one of you heard the shot. To recognize? To locate?"

Nobody had.

"Not even something you thought was a backfire?"

"Not," Pam said, "to pick out from everything else. That is, probably we all heard it but not really. If you see what I mean."

Foley looked at Pearson. Upsetting experience this lady had had, seeing a friend shot right in front of her, having to notify his widow. Not used to things like that. "Sure," Pearson said. "Happens that way all the time. Well—"

"No reason to keep you four here," Foley said. "Somebody got your names?"

Somebody had.

"Just in case," Pearson said. "Well—"

"Bill!" Pamela North said. "We're over here."

William Weigand, captain of detectives, Homicide, Manhattan West, came across the small and pleasant lobby. He stopped in front of them and looked down.

"What's this I hear?" Bill Weigand said. "You've had another author shot out from under you, Jerry?"

Gerald North nodded his head, gloomily.

"Hell of a way to run a publishing house," Bill Weigand said.

3

Captain William Weigand, in his small office in West Twentieth Street, had been about to call it a day, since even policemen must sometimes call a day a day. The report, coming to him as a matter of routine, that there had been another sniper victim, and this one dead, had not at first seemed sufficient reason to start the day over. It had been a long day already and had ended, satisfactorily, with an arrest—Antonio Spagalenti had not, after all, been in his office when his wife was strangled in their apartment in lower Manhattan. It did not appear to be true that the scratches on his face had been inflicted by the family cat. The Medical Examiner's laboratory reported that Mrs. Spagalenti had scratched someone. And it was easy enough to prove that Antonio Spagalenti had found a new interest in life, and a blond one.

Another sniping, and particularly a fatal one, was certainly unpleasant. It was, however, a thing which the precinct detective squad, with the precinct uniformed force, could handle as well as anyone, which probably was not going to be too satisfactorily, and no reflections on anybody. If Homicide West needed to get into it, Lieutenant Stein could lead it in. Stein had arrived when due, and been told, "Nothing but this, John," and shown "this." "Sniper killed, this time. Killed a man named—"

Bill Weigand had had to look again at the report to give Lieutenant John Stein the name. The victims of snipers are impersonal, being merely unlucky. "Anthony Payne," Weigand read. "Seems to have been a writer of some—"

Bill Weigand stopped so abruptly that Stein looked at him almost anxiously. Bill Weigand said, "Damn it to hell," using half his voice, the other half having, somehow, lost itself.

He did not know a man named Anthony Payne. But he and his wife Dorian had been invited to a cocktail party being given in celebration of the publication of a new book by an Anthony Payne and—if Antonio Spagalenti had really been scratched by the family cat—might well have gone. Invited by North Books, Inc., formally, with an informal comment: "Dinner after? G.N." Party at—Bill checked his mind. Hotel Dumont. He looked again at the report he still held out to Lieutenant Stein. Payne had been killed in front of the Dumont.

Sergeant Aloysius Mullins had already called it a day. He would, for a few hours more, be spared the knowledge. Deputy Chief Inspector Artemus O'Malley was presumably at home. He would have to know. He would turn alarming red; he would, without doubt, shout, "Not again!" O'Malley would scream, in agony, "Not those *Norths* again!" He did not have instantly to know. Tomorrow the news could be broken, gently.

There was nobody on the sidewalk when Weigand reached the Hotel Dumont. There were several police cars around; there was a section of the sidewalk closed to pedestrians. Weigand went into the Dumont's lobby. He heard his name spoken in a raised, familiar voice. They were over there. They were indeed.

Now, half an hour later, they were a few blocks away, at the Hotel Algonquin, having dinner—four of them: the Norths and Weigand, a man named Tom Hathaway, to whom, after he had been identified, Bill had said, "Might help if you could come along, Hathaway. If you're not tied up." Hathaway had not been.

It remained, Bill told them, a hundred to one that it was not Payne, as Payne, who had been killed. A man who happened to be named Payne, happened to be a moderately celebrated (Gerald North and Tom Hathaway had looked at each other a little gloomily at the modification) author, had also happened to be a target for a crackpot with a gun.

"He wasn't wearing a hat," Pam said. "His head—well, I suppose it would have stood out a bit. Like a—well, it would shine of course—I mean—"

"Payne was very bald," Jerry said. "That's what she means."

"Well," Pam said, "one has to take things into account. That is, there they are, aren't they?"

The point, to get back to it, was that it was only incidental that Payne was Payne. Hence, whatever might have happened at the party had nothing to do with what had happened after the party. So precinct had as good a chance as anyone; routine would serve if anything would serve. And routine was in progress. Foley and Pearson, and other detectives and uniformed men were going doggedly at it—were going, in the Dumont and the King Arthur opposite, from front room to front room, identifying, briefly questioning, guests who were in their rooms; sniffing, searching, in empty rooms. The smell of cordite lingers; it was hardly likely that a rifle—probably target, with telescopic sight; probably .22 calibre—would be found leaning against a wall, but one never knows until one looks. There were hotels—tall and narrow and elderly, like the Dumont itself—on either side of the Dumont. They, also, had rooms with windows on the street— many rooms. There was another hotel on one side of the King Arthur. On the other side of the King Arthur there was an office building and parking garage, with a roof. Snipers often use roofs. Now and then, although not often enough, they leave cartridge cases behind them. Once in a hundred times or so there may be identifiable fingerprints on cartridge cases. One never knows until one looks. It takes a long time to look in all possible places.

"All the same," Pam said, bringing them again back to it, "he knocked Gardner Willings down. Mr. Willings wasn't pleased. Mr. Willings isn't used to things like that."

The statement was made for the record, rather than as an offer of information. They all knew Willings— knew of Willings. Every literate American knew of Gardner Willings. He hunted big game in Africa and had been photographed often with a foot on it. He had written about Africa. He had been, until recently, a sports-car racer. He had written about sports-car racing. He was flamboyant. Now and then he spoke of himself in the third person. And if he was not a great writer, he was so near it as made no difference until, as was so often said, time had told. About his influence on American writing there could be no doubt whatever.

"Nowadays, every American who doesn't try to write like Hemingway tries to write like Willings," one critic had said, which was saying it flatly, and in which there was unmistakable truth.

Gardner Willings, in short, was not a man who would like to be knocked down.

And there was, of course, another point: Gardner Willings was a notable rifle shot. Lions and tigers without number, and a rhinoceros here and there, could be brought to testify, if ghostly testimony were admissible. (And, of course, subject to translation.)

"All the same," Bill Weigand said, "it sounds a bit preposterous, doesn't it? Grant he was annoyed—"

"Unless," Pam said. "Before he was shot, poor Mr. Payne kept saying that Willings must be crazy. And there's something about that somewhere—great something is—"

" 'Great wits are sure to madness near allied,' " Jerry said. "Dryden."

"So terribly literate," Pam said, fondly. "On the other hand, I thought that Willings had merely too much taken. And Mr. Payne, poor man, was a bit of a twerp, all things considered."

She was looked at, waited for.

"Not evidence," Pam said. "One woman's opinion. And I'm not impartial. I don't like his books."

Jerry sighed.

"This new one," Pam said. "It's called *The Liberated*. It ought to be called, *The Dismembered*." She looked at Jerry. "Which you know perfectly well," she said. "Where was I?"

"Admit a spot of torture here and there," Jerry said. "A bit of sadism. We don't offer it as a juvenile."

"Catering," Pam said. "I won't say pandering." She paused to consider. "On the other hand," Pam said, "I will say pandering."

"By all means," Jerry said.

"Please, you two," Bill Weigand said. "Why a twerp? Only because you don't like his books?"

"He acted like a twerp," Pam said. "I don't mean by knocking Mr. Willings down. I think that was pretty much an accident, anyway. Don't you, Jerry? And—wasn't he a twerp? Tom won't send it out as a release."

Jerry thought for some seconds.

"All right," he said. "His review of Willings's book was vicious. Over and above the call of duty. Malicious and—jealous. Envious."

"Twerpish."

"If you like. And, for what it's worth, he wasn't precisely—intrepid—when Willings came at him. No special reason to be intrepid. Only—" He looked at Pam.

"He wrote intrepid," Pam said. "In *I Know Africa.*"

"*The Africa I Know,*" Jerry said. "Yes. The conquering-hero type. Facing down enraged natives."

"I've never blamed the natives," Pam said. "He was a twerp. And somebody asked me to tell him to drop dead." She stopped abruptly. She had not been thinking of, talking of, the Anthony Payne of flesh and blood. Particularly of blood. An abstraction is all very well. A man, alive seconds before, dying bloodily on a sidewalk— Everything seemed, momentarily, to waiver.

"All right, Pam," Jerry said, and reached out and put a hand on hers. "All right, girl."

"I'm sorry," Pam said. "All at once I—"

"I know."

The wavering of everything ended.

"Who," Bill Weigand said, "said that? Asked that?"

"A man named Lars something," Pam said. "He—wait a minute. Lars Simon. He adapted *Uprising.*

41

Made a play of it. And—he was very annoyed at Mr. Payne. Seemed to be. Perhaps it was just—theater people dramatize. I met him and—"

She told, briefly, of meeting Lars Simon; of his, perhaps dramatized, attitude toward Anthony Payne. Bill Weigand looked at Jerry.

Jerry had heard something about it; heard from Livingston Birdwood. Simon was not only the author of the play version of *Uprising*. He was also directing the play. He felt that Payne had been "horning in"; interfering not only with the dramatization itself, but with the direction. Even with selection of the cast, Simon had complained to Birdwood. He had told Birdwood that, if it kept on, Birdwood might have to get himself another boy.

"Only a squabble," Jerry said. "At any rate, Birdwood thought so. A case of Simon getting tensed up. As, he says, Simon has a habit of getting. He did say—Birdwood, I mean—that he was keeping his fingers crossed. He said that all producers end up with permanently bent fingers."

"He did get one of the actors fired," Tom Hathaway said. "Payne did. Anyway, that's what I've heard. Made a thing of it. Said this guy—name of Blaine something—was n.b.g. A row about it, and Birdwood made Simon give in. I don't know why. You'd think if Simon wanted—"

"Payne put some money in the play," Jerry said. "I don't know how much or whether—"

"Blaine who?" Pam said. She spoke very quickly. "Smythe? With a 'y' and, for that matter, an 'e'?"

That sounded right to Tom Hathaway.

"Because—" Pam said, "unless there are two of him, and there seldom are, of course, he and Mrs. Payne are very—anyway—"

She told them of Lauren Payne on the sofa at the party; of her feeling that there was anxiety in Lauren Payne's manner, and in her eyes. "He seemed—" Pam said, and hesitated. "So often," she said, "people remember more than there was. When there's reason to remember. I think now he was—seemed—protective. And that they seemed—close together. But I didn't think that—I don't think I thought that—until Mr. Payne was killed."

"I know," Bill Weigand said. "It happens that way. Still—"

"From what I heard," Tom Hathaway said, "Lars Simon thought this Smythe was very good in the part. And Payne didn't make his pitch until—well, until pretty well on. They've been rehearsing for quite a while. Lot of rewriting, apparently. Which louses things up."

"Anxious?" Bill said. "Mrs. Payne?"

"Well—any word, I guess. Jittery. Perhaps even—" Pam hesitated. "Perhaps even frightened," Pam said. "She's very sensitive, I think. When I—when Jerry made me be the one to tell her—" She stopped again; looked at Jerry.

"I thought a woman," Jerry said. "There didn't seem to be anybody else."

"Oh," Pam said, "I know the convention. Anyway—it hit her very hard. Terribly hard. It was as if—as if everything had fallen away. So if you—all right, all of us—are drawing inferences about her and this Blaine Smythe—when she was told her husband was dead things fell apart for her. I'm sure of—" But, suddenly, she paused. "Of course that's what it was," she said, very firmly—very firmly indeed.

"Unless," Bill Weigand said, and spoke gently, "she thought Smythe had killed him."

"You were the one who said it, Bill," Pam said. "That he was—was a target. Not Anthony Payne."

"That that seemed probable. It still does. Simon wished Payne would take a trip around the world. Or, drop dead. You felt there was a—call it relationship—between Payne's wife and this actor named Smythe. What else, Pam? In case Payne wasn't merely a target?"

"It's all—trivial. It all seemed trivial. There was a man named Self. Very contemptuous of Mr. Payne. Works in—"

"James Self. Runs a bookstore," Jerry said. "Does a little criticism on the side. Very select criticism for very select readers. Very—superior. Particularly to authors who sell. Harmless, so far as I know. Anyway—I can't see him criticizing with a rifle."

"There was the first Mrs. Payne," Pam said. "Faith Constable she is now. In the play—the one Mr. Simon's doing. She said Mr. Payne had a 'dear, dirty little mind.' But not as if she cared."

Hathaway laughed, briefly. He had done publicity for Faith Constable a few years before. He doubted very much whether she minded the condition of Payne's mind, or ever had.

"Married years ago," Hathaway said. "Not for long. Perhaps two years. She divorced—Reno type. I'd guess because she thought Payne wasn't going anywhere. Thirty years ago he wasn't." He turned for confirmation to Jerry North.

Thirty years before, Payne had shown no great indication that he was going anywhere. He had written one novel, about life—his life, too obviously—in a small Ohio town. Published; sale of possibly two thousand. He had, after several years—and after Faith—written another, about an actress married to a strug-

44

gling young writer, and throwing him aside as an impediment. Quite bitter, in a still childish fashion. Sales not quite as good as the first. North Books, Inc., had published neither, not then being in existence.

Payne had then, for some years, worked on a magazine staff, with a few by-lines; setting no pages afire; proffering no more novels. He had gone to Africa on an assignment; he had discoverd Africa. "Sometimes," Jerry said, "he seemed to feel he'd invented it. Or, at least, staked it out. Willings had an earlier claim, of course."

"And," Pam said, "wrote better books."

Nobody denied that.

"All the same," Jerry said, "Payne's first African book helped when we could use help. So—"

"He married again, along there some time," Hathaway said. "At least, when I was getting stuff a while back for a new biography, he said something about his second wife. I thought he meant Lauren, and said something which showed it, and he said, 'No, I don't mean Lauren. My second.' I waited and he said, 'Skip it.' So I skipped it."

They were finishing coffee by then. They were, by then, almost alone in the Oak Room.

Bill Weigand regarded his empty coffee cup, without seeing it. It did appear that, at the party, there had been several people who shared Pam's view that Anthony Payne was something of a twerp. A man who was merely "contemptuous." A man who thought it would be pleasant if Payne dropped dead. A woman who thought Payne had had a "dirty little mind," but had not seemed concerned about this. A woman who had appeared to Pam to be upset, possibly frightened. Of her husband? A writer who had wanted Payne to eat his words, in indigestible form, and been humiliated, made to appear ridiculous. Still—still the chances were high that a target had been hit, only incidentally a man.

"Jerry," Pam said, "did you do something to a busboy? To make him hate you?"

"Busboy?"

"Thin. Dark. Picking up used glasses. In a white jacket with a dark patch on the shoulder. From trays. A—"

"Do something to?" Jerry ran the fingers of his right hand through his hair. "What on earth would I do to a busboy?"

"There's that," Pam said. "So it must have been Mr. Payne. You were together—it was before Willings—and he—the busboy—stood and glared at you. At both of you, that is. As if he hated."

Briefly, she gave details. Jerry shook his head. Jerry hadn't noticed, hadn't felt a glare. So far as he could remember, Payne had showed no consciousness of being glared at.

"Of course," Pam said, "it could be he didn't like any of us. That all of us were just a bunch of dirty glasses. If I were a busboy I'd feel that way, I think. With other people having fun. But still—"

They separated outside the Algonquin, the Norths going downtown to their apartment; Tom Hathaway uptown to his.

It was, Bill Weigand thought, now more than time to call it a day. But, since he was only a few blocks from the Dumont, since things would still be going on there, he might as well see what had gone on. Not that anything was expected. But still, as Pam North had said.

4

Captain Jonathan Frank, commanding, Fourth Detective District, was talking to the desk clerk at the Hotel Dumont. Weigand waited. Frank said, "Fifth floor, and you're sure on the street side? About half an hour after the—occurrence—and was in a hurry?" The clerk said, "Yes, but I told you—"

"Sure," Frank said. "Catching a plane to Frisco and cutting it fine. You told me. What he said. Sure, I know that's all you've got to go on. Nobody blames you. Hi, Bill."

Bill Weigand said, "Hi, Johnny."

"Twelve floors," Frank said. *"And* the roof. Just in this one. Five front rooms to the floor so we come up with sixty rooms, and cross off the permanents—only why?—and you come up with fifty-four. Of which one is an old lady in a wheel chair, sure, but she's got a companion. And across the street—" He shrugged. He spread his hands.

"Right," Bill said. "And nobody saw anything or

47

heard anything, and none of the rooms smells of powder and—"

"Snipers," Frank said, with great weariness. "Crackpots. Some time we'll wake up. Quit making guns except for cops. Make possession of all guns illegal. Make the manufacture of ammo illegal."

"And," Bill said, "abolish roofs. Allow no windows facing streets."

"Very funny, Bill," Frank said. "Your brain trust interested? In a crackpot sniping?"

"Not if it is," Bill said, and was told, sure it was, and then looked at.

"This party," Jonathan Frank said, "that friend of yours gave it? North?"

"Yes."

"Oh," Frank said. "The ruckus. Be very pat. Only, Willings's room isn't on the front. One gets you a hundred it was a loony."

"No bet, Johnny. Willings does stay here?"

"Does now. Checked in three or four days ago. Expects to be here about a week. Didn't bring a rifle with him, far's anybody noticed. Of course, nobody brought a rifle with him. They all tell us that. Only, somebody brought a rifle with him. On account, nobody spit a bullet into Payne." Frank sighed. "I was taking the wife to the movies," he said. He scrutinized Bill Weigand's face again, with greater care. "You got something, Bill?"

"Bits and pieces. Odds and ends. Several people at the party didn't like Payne too much, I'm told."

"By those friends of yours?"

"By those friends of mine."

"Happens Willings is in the bar now," Frank said. "I—"

The clerk said, "Telephone call, Captain. In booth one."

"—was thinking of having a little chat with him," Frank said. "You want to, Bill? . . ."

"The Bottom of the Well," so named because a writer who frequented it had once said that that was where he always felt he was, in a small, high barroom, with dark green walls. It does not at any time accommodate many, and when Bill Weigand went in it accommodated only three—a couple at a corner table; a large man with a red beard on a stool at the bar. "Only rum worth drinking," the red-bearded man was telling the barman when Bill sat down beside him. Gardner Willings had a heavy voice, with something of a rumble in it. "Good rum," Willings said, and sipped from a tall glass. Bill ordered scotch and water. He said, "Mr. Willings?"

"Don't autograph," Willings said. "Why should I?"

"No reason," Bill said. "I'm a police officer. Name of Weigand."

"I was off balance," Willings said. "Slipped on something. The two-bit phony couldn't punch his way out of a paper bag."

He turned on his stool and looked at Bill Weigand. He had a square face under the red beard; he had light blue eyes. He was a very large man.

"What's it to you, anyway?" Willings said.

"Payne's dead."

"So I heard. Late on, for my money. Service to American letters. Like to shake the hand that fired the shot." The pale blue eyes were very intent. It occurred to Bill Weigand that he had never seen eyes quite like Willings's. He had the slightly uncomfortable feeling that the light blue eyes were looking into his mind.

"Which wouldn't be with myself," Willings said. "People say I do. Say I pat myself on the back. Perhaps. Not this time." He shifted his gaze, looked at Bill's drink. "Pallid stuff," he said. "Ought to drink rum. Virgin Islands rum." He turned back to Bill. "I didn't shoot the son of a bitch, he said. "Not worth the trouble."

"You didn't like him, obviously."

"Lots of people I don't like. Lots of things I don't like. There are good things and bad things, and he was a bad thing. He was a fake, and I don't like fakes. *The Africa I Know*." He used a short, explicit word. He whirled on his stool toward the couple in the corner. "Sorry, lady," he said.

"Oh," the girl said, "I've heard the word, Mr. Willings. I've heard a lot of words."

Willlings turned back to Bill Weigand.

"There you have it," he said. "Honest girl. Mealy-mouthed bunch ride herd. But everybody knows the words. When a word's a good word for what you want to say, you ought to use the word. Right?"

"Right," Bill said.

"You're thinking about that review I was going to make him eat. It was a stinker. Also, it was a lousy job. The man couldn't write. You read it, I suppose?"

Bill shook his head.

"I'll be damned," Willings said. He seemed entirely surprised. "Everybody read it."

"I didn't, Mr. Willings—after this—incident. At the party. By the way, did you come to the party with that in mind?"

"What else? Heard about the party. Thought it might be fun. Getting Payne to eat, I mean. Long as I was there, I thought I might have a couple." For the first time he smiled slightly. "A couple made the idea seem very good," he said. "So I had a couple more. Idea seemed fine. I wasn't drunk. I don't get drunk." He finished his long rum drink. He patted the base of the glass against the bar. The barman took the glass away and began to mix.

"After the incident," Bill said. "What did you do?"

"Went up to my room. Had a nap. I sleep when it seems like a good idea. Didn't know about somebody's good deed for the day until about half an hour ago."

"You'd known Payne for some time?"

"You're a funny copper," Willings said. "What are you after?"

"Anything I can get."

"I'm the wrong tree to bark up. But—yes. Donkey's years."

"Disliking him all the time?"

"More or less. What difference does that make? You only see people you like?"

"I see all kinds."

"Probably do," Willings said. "So do I. In some ways, ours is the same trade. Find out about people. You put them in jail. I put them in books. I used Payne a couple of times. Remember Ponsby in my *Turn at the Bridge?*"

Bill remembered the title; only the title. He shook his head.

"Read it, didn't you?"

Bill shook his head again.

"My God," Willings said. "You *can* read?"

It sounded to Bill Weigand as if Willings really wanted to know, really wanted to resolve a doubt. Bill said, "Yes, I can read. Your character Ponsby was Anthony Payne?"

"Publicly, I deny it," Willings said.

"Did he recognize himself?"

"As the chaser the girls laughed at? Sure he did. So he tried to put me into *Uprising*. Couldn't swing it, of course. Not up to it."

"He was a chaser?"

"And how."

"They did laugh?"

"The bright ones. Faith did. Laughed him out of her life." He drank. "Not all," he said. "There're always half-wits."

"His present wife. Widow. She's one of the ones who didn't laugh?"

Willings shrugged his heavy shoulders and turned to his drink. It occurred to Bill Weigand that he had begun to bore the—justly—famous Mr. Willings. It is the fate of a policeman to bore many.

"No laughing matter, being married to Payne," Willings said, into his rum drink. "How would I know? Don't know the lady."

Which seemed to take care of that.

"Met her couple of years ago," Willings said. "Came down to the islands and looked us up. More damn people look us up. Thought, 'Poor gal doesn't know what she's in for.' Thought, 'Too tender for the bastard.' Thought, 'Shame to waste her on the two-bit phony.' Only met her that once. Had Sally use the gag, after that. 'Willings is at work,' with proper awe. Good at it, Sally is. Hear her, and you'd swear she believed it. Well?"

The last seemed to toss something into the air. Bill was not entirely sure what.

"She's a good-looking gal," Willings said, himself catching whatever it was he had tossed. (Sally, whoever Sally might be, or Mrs. Anthony Payne?) "Tender. Also, she's got money. Could be why the bastard married her, couldn't it? Not that I've anything against their having money. One of mine had money, you remember. Samantha, that was. Money's a good thing to have."

Weigand remembered nothing about Samantha, never having heard of her before. There seemed no use in mentioning this to Willings, who clearly thought that all the world would remember Samantha, who would have acquired fame by osmosis. To those who had much to do with Gardner Willings it must sometimes be hard to remember that Willings *was* the institution he took himself to be, or close to it.

"However," Willings said, "I wasn't thinking of Lauren particularly. He had this new one, you know. Pretty little thing and I'd guess about twenty. Tender. Half-witted, of course, or she'd have seen through him. But—tender. Too young to laugh. Not bright enough. But—pretty as hell."

Bill Weigand waited. Willings seemed, now, entirely ready to keep himself going. Willings is willing, Bill Weigand thought, and rather wished he hadn't.

"Couple of nights ago," Willings said. "Having dinner with a man named Self. Starting some sort of magazine. Good stuff. Stuff nobody'll want. Wants me to do something for it. *Me*." He paused, apparently in wonderment. "And I may," Willings said. "Just may. Nice kid, this Self boy. Reminds me of—" He stopped and drank and, for a moment, looked beyond the drink, at nothing—at the past.

"Anyway," Willings said, "Payne came in with this girl—little dark girl with big dark eyes. Looking at the bastard with—" He paused. "As if her eyes saw greatness," he said. "The poor, pretty, benighted little idiot. And Self started to stand up. Damn near knocked the table over. And then, just sat down again and looked at them. Good scene, and some time I'll do it the way it ought to be done. Confrontation, see?"

"Right," Bill said. "Because the girl was with Payne?"

"What else? His girl. Looking that way at this pink dome of nothing at all. Suddenly, his hands full of dust."

"He say something to tell you that?"

Willings turned and looked at Bill Weigand, and with surprise. His look, Bill thought, is to say that I'm even dumber than he had thought. But when Willings spoke it was with resignation.

"No," he said. "Said nothing. I see things, copper. It was the way I saw it."

"Right," Bill said. "This Self—James Self? I thought he ran a bookstore."

"He runs a bookstore. Runs a bookstore. Writes reviews for—oh, *Partisan Review*. Gets out a magazine of his own. The poor bastard can't write, you see." There was a note of deep sorrow in Willings's heavy voice, as he mentioned, with a kind of awe, this most tragic of human predicaments. "Got to do something." He finished his drink and looked at his empty glass. He shook his head at it. He said, "You know Self?"

"Heard of him today," Bill said. "He was at the party here."

"Girl with him?"

Bill didn't know.

"Didn't see him," Willings said. "Hell of a lot of nobodies. As you'd expect. Why does anybody give a party like that?"

"I don't know," Bill said, and reached the bottom of his own glass and stood up. "You'll be in town a few days?"

"Probably. Why?"

"We like to know where people are."

"I didn't kill the bastard. Not worth the trouble."

Bill Weigand said, "Right," and went out of "The Bottom of the Well." It was, he thought, mildly interesting that Gardner Willings had, more or less unprompted, brought up the "confrontation" scene which had involved James Self and a pretty dark girl with big dark eyes. And Anthony Payne. A small present to a deserving policeman? Present of small red herring?

Call it a night, now. Bill went out of the Hotel Dumont. On the sidewalk, Captain Jonathan Frank said, "Hey!" to him. Frank looked pleased. "Got him?" Bill said, and Frank, his voice sounding pleased, said it looked like it.

"Hiding on the roof," he said, and pointed across the street toward the Hotel King Arthur. "Tried to make a run for it, and one of the boys had to stop him. Knocked him out, sort of. But he'll come around, O.K."

"Sure," Bill said. "So that's that."

"Looks like it," Frank said. "Lucky break. Find out where he ditched the gun, and we're in."

5

From the bedroom there came the cry of a Siamese cat in agony. "Then you feel," Dave Garroway said, from a twenty-three-inch screen, in a tone of anxiety, "that we tend to underestimate the menace of communism here at home?" "It's frightening," the author of *The Unseen Menace* said, and Dave Garroway looked properly frightened. "Of atheistic communism?" Garroway said, getting it clear, and the author said, "I'm afraid that's true, Dave." Garroway looked at the camera, and it was clear to Pam North that he was scared stiff. From the bedroom the cat wailed.

Mr. Garroway's such a nice man, Pam thought. So—she paused for the word. The word came. "Sincere." Precisely the right word. The cat wailed. It was clear that the cat was undergoing torture.

"Here, Shadow," Pam said. "She's out here."

The cat named Shadow had lost the cat named Stilts. Stilts was lying on the floor at Pam's feet. When Shadow wailed first, Stilts lifted her head and listened.

Then she put her head down again. Nothing wrong with her, the movement said. Silly cat, but not in any trouble.

There was the quick click of cat claws on the hall's bare floor. Shadow appeared, crying. She looked at Pam and wailed. "There," Pam said, and pointed. Shadow ran to Stilts, rubbed against Stilts, began to purr loudly. Stilts licked her, perfunctorily. Shadow licked back with eager excitement. Stilts turned slightly and hit Shadow in the face. Shadow laid her ears back and leaped into an embrace with Stilts. It seemed to Pam, watching, that Stilts sighed. Unquestionably, Stilts pushed. Shadow began to cry on a quite different note—in the tone of a cat about to eat another cat for breakfast.

Stilts, with a sudden flowing movement, stood up and knocked Shadow down. Then she sat and began to wash behind the ears. Shadow looked at her. Shadow sat and washed behind the ears.

"You poor dear," Pam said to Shadow, "are you going to be a kitten always?"

Shadow leaped to Pam's lap and Pam stroked her. It was a bit, Pam thought, like stroking an eel only, of course, furrier. Shadow purred. By decibels the loudest purrer we've ever had, Pam thought, and said, "Nice baby."

Stilts watched for a moment. She lay down on the carpet again, and this time put one paw over her eyes.

No two of them are ever alike, Pam thought. She pressed the proper area of remote control and Dave Garroway, still looking frightened, vanished. Which was odd when one considered how much alike these two seal-points looked. Shadow's eyes were perceptibly larger and, for that matter, bluer. She was a long, low cat, shaped a good deal—a good deal too much, if one chose to be critical—like a dachshund. (This com-

parison was never made, audibly, in her presence.)
Shadow was constantly losing something, usually
Stilts, and mourning loudly. People who were always
talking of the detached self-reliance of cats should
meet Shadow. If, of course, Shadow could, on en-
countering strangers, be got out from underneath
whatever was nearest.

Shadow was almost a year old, and at a year a cat is
a cat, ready to follow a cat's trade. In the country, that
summer, Shadow had pursued, and missed, butter-
flies. Stilts, who was a little over two, had brought
home moles, mice, chipmunks and a medium-sized
rabbit. (The one, it was to be hoped, who had got
under the fence and eaten the lettuce or, at the least, a
near relative of the one.)

Stilts was a cat who walked tall; she was, save for
slightly crossed eyes, everything a Siamese ought to
be. She had been given to the Norths by a sympathetic
veterinarian, who—Pam suspected with the Norths in
mind—had accepted her from owners who explained
that they were ordered to Argentina. All the veterinarian knew of her was that she was a pretty, friendly cat.
One of the things he did not know about her was that
she was pregnant and another that she had not been
inoculated.

When she returned from the hospital, a wraith, after
parturition and enteritis, in that order, she found
Shadow—then nameless; then of a shape and texture
which had almost led to her being called Cushion—
under a sofa. "Larger than I would have expected,"
Stilts clearly thought, "but one of my kittens." Stilts,
who had evidently been fearless from the day she was
born, enticed Shadow from under, explained that cats
do not need to hide from people and washed her
thoroughly. She earned a slave who was sometimes
clearly a nuisance, but one to be tolerated by a gentle

cat. Her slave, who had been on order when Stilts was offered, had a long pedigree and quite perceptible tabby markings on her rather thickish tail.

"The baby," Pam North said, fondly, to the ecstatic purrer on her lap. The telephone rang. Stilts jumped up instantly and danced away to answer it. Shadow, watching her, wailed at this new desertion.

The voice was very low, almost husky. It was carefully controlled—so carefully, Pam thought, as to have in its texture a certain unreality. Pam said, "Why, of course. Whenever you like," and listened a moment longer and said, "That'll be fine," and put the receiver back. For a moment she sat at the telephone table and looked at the olive-green telephone. What did Lauren Payne want, want anxiously, to talk to her about? At—Pam looked at the watch on her wrist— five minutes before nine?

Pam went to the bedroom, followed by cats. Pam spread up both beds—and had to reopen one of them to extricate Stilts, who had got herself spread in. Pam changed from housecoat to a gray-blue dress and had just finished lipstick when the door chimes sounded. Stilts rushed to answer the door. Shadow went under one of the beds.

Lauren Payne wore a woolen sheath, and was a woman who could wear a sheath. She wore mink over it, and Pam, admiringly, thought "Phew." She was a slender, graceful woman, a little taller than Pam herself. The color of the sheath was a little deeper than the copper of Lauren Payne's hair, the flickering copper in her greenish eyes. Very lovely, as Pam remembered her. Her low-pitched voice very steady, as it had been on the telephone. She was afraid she was being a nuisance. Her lips smiled. Her eyes did not. There was strain in her eyes.

Seated in a deep chair in the living room, Lauren

Payne hardly knew where to begin. It would seem to Mrs. North— "What a pretty cat. A Siamese, isn't she? Such very blue eyes. A really beautiful cat."

"We think so," Pam said, giving all the time needed. "Some people like them fluffy, of course. We feel that fluff hides cat. And there are the knots and—"

Lauren Payne was not listening. Pam North let cats drift away.

"When you came to tell me Anthony was—had been shot," Lauren said without looking at Pam, and then did look at her. "It was kind of you. It's a hard thing to do." She paused. "What did I say, Mrs. North?"

"Why—" Pam said, and paused to remember.

"I'd taken something," Lauren said. "A sedative. I was—groggy, I guess. And then, afterward, the doctor gave me something else. The thing is—in between it's rather like a dream. A dream I half remember."

"Why—" Pam said again. "You were lying down. You said to come in and—"

"Just you. There wasn't anybody else?"

"Not right away. Then the doctor came. I said I was afraid I had bad news—I said something dreadful had happened. I don't know the precise words. Then— well, then I merely told you. That Mr. Payne had been shot and that he was dead. And you—"

Lauren leaned forward in the deep chair. It seemed to Pam that her eyes said, "Hurry. *Hurry!*"

"For a moment," Pam said, "I thought you hadn't heard me. Then you said—I'm not sure I remember it precisely. You said, 'Anthony? Not *Anthony?*' and I said something meaningless—that I was sorry. Something like that. You looked at me for a moment—you don't remember this?"

"No. Go on. Please go on."

"But," Pam said, "there wasn't anything—not really anything. I think you said, 'No. Oh—*no!*' Something like that. And put your hands up to your forehead. You'd been lying down. You were sitting up by then. I don't remember that I said anything. I think I put my arm around your shoulders. Then you said, 'Shot? You said he was shot?' It was something like that. Not really as if you expected me to say it again. Then you said—asked if we—no, 'they'—'knew.' I supposed, who had shot Mr. Payne, and I said, 'No. Nobody knows yet,' and then that the shot seemed to have come from above somewhere. I think I said it was probably a sniper. One of those insane—"

"I know," Lauren said. "That was all I said? Nothing about—anybody?"

"Why," Pam said, "you said his name—your husband's. As if you couldn't believe it. I don't know what—"

"Nothing else?"

Pam went through her mind. She didn't remember anything else. After Lauren had covered her eyes, after Pam had moved beside her and put a steadying arm around shaking shoulders, Lauren had made only low, wordless sounds, moaning sounds. "I'm sure that's all," Pam said. "Then the doctor came and gave you something and—got somebody to be with you for a while. A nurse—somebody."

"Not a nurse," Lauren said. "One of the housekeepers. An assistant housekeeper, I think it was. A woman—a very nice woman—named—" She shook her head. "Mason," she said. "Something like that. It doesn't matter. I went to sleep quite soon, I think." She leaned back in the deep chair and closed her eyes. "You'll think—I don't know what you'll think," she said, and spoke slowly, from a distance, in a voice which no longer, to Pam's ears, sounded so carefully guarded. "To come to a complete stranger this way. Ask about what I ought to remember myself."

"It was a terrible shock," Pam said. "A terrible thing to happen. I don't wonder you—"

"You see," Lauren said, as if Pam had not spoken. (As I might as well not have, Pam thought. Since I said nothing.) "You see, I—with Anthony gone—there isn't anybody. I'm—I feel terribly alone. That's it, really. I—I couldn't just sit in that awful room. The room I'd—I'd heard it in. I had to—well, just talk, I guess. To somebody. And you—you were kind last night."

"Nothing," Pam said. "I only—"

"That was all it was," Lauren said. "A—just an impulse." She leaned forward in the chair and smiled again—smiled again with lips, still did not smile with eyes. "You'll have to forgive me."

"Oh. As for that? You mean, literally, you haven't anybody to turn to?"

"Literally," Lauren said. She smiled again. "It's not so terrible," she said. "I'm a grown woman. Just at the moment, with Anthony gone—I feel—I suppose the word is bereft."

It seemed to Pam that, now, manner had returned to the voice; that voice was too carefully considered, words (for all the seeming stumbling over them) most carefully chosen. And Pam found that she did not think that "bereft" was, really, quite the word. Not the word to use of one's self. Still, of course—

"But," Pam said, "you must have friends."

Lauren shook her head. She said, "Acquaintances. Anthony is—was—always so busy. And so often away getting material. We had very little—" She ended with a shrug of delicate shoulders.

And in Pam's mind, in spite of her best intentions, three words formed— "Oh, come now."

"That Mr. Smythe," Pam said. "Blaine Smythe? I thought he seemed—"

Lauren said, "Oh," in a certain way—a way which dismissed Blaine Smythe. "A friend of Anthony's," she said. "Not of mine, really. One of the actors in Anthony's play. Anthony met him at rehearsals, I suppose. I hardly know him."

This time Pam almost spoke the same three words. She remembered Lauren and Blaine Smythe sitting on a sofa in the Dumont's Gold Room, of Smythe leaning toward the slender and lovely (and strangely nervous, uneasy) woman and talking, with what had looked like intent earnestness, to her.

"I've bothered you long enough," Lauren said. "I'm sure you have things to do."

"No," Pam said. "Oh—things. Not really things, though. You know."

Lauren Payne did not look as if she did.

"Mrs. Payne," Pam said, "what did you think you might have said. And forgotten saying?"

(What were you *afraid* you might have said? And fogotten saying?)

"Goodness," Lauren said. "I didn't have the faintest. That was it. I thought you understood that. I just—there was a gap. It disturbed me a little. That was all."

(Oh, come now.)

"And," Lauren said, "it's been dear of you, and I feel so much better, just having a chance to—to talk. Even if I didn't make much sense."

She got out of the deep chair. Her movement was without effort, remarkable for grace. Not frail at all, obviously. Whatever one thought on seeing her first. Lithe, if one came to that.

"The more I think of it," Lauren said, and smiled again and this time held out a slender hand, "the more I think my barging in this way was quite unforgivable."

Pam shook her head. Lauren Payne's expressive

face changed suddenly. It seemed to droop, to lose contours.

"It's all so meaningless," Lauren said, and spoke slowly. "So—so horribly without meaning. Somebody—somebody half crazy—shoots a gun, just—just to shoot a gun—and kills somebody like Anthony." She put both hands to her forehead, covering her eyes. She held them there a moment, took them down, said, "I'm sorry. But it would almost have been better—" She broke off. "The police do think it was that, don't they? What they call a sniper?"

"I suppose so," Pam said. "At least—yes, I suppose they do."

"Somebody they'll never catch. It's all so meaningless."

Pam thought of several things to say. What she said was, "Yes."

Stilts accompanied Mrs. Lauren Payne to the apartment door, and would have gone farther with her if Pam had been less quick. The door closed, Pam put the dancing cat on the floor and spoke to her.

"What," Pam asked her dancing cat, "was she afraid she had said? Doesn't she know her husband got Blaine Smythe fired, and that I can tell casual acquaintance from something else whatever the direction of the wind? And if she wants to know what the police think, why doesn't she ask the police? Because she knows we're friends of Bill Weigand?"

"Yow-ough?" Stilts said.

"You may well ask," Pam North said.

There was no point in wasting further time on the case of Anthony Payne, deceased. There were, certainly, aspects of interest. Mr. Payne had, it appeared, given several persons cause to dislike him, most obviously a burly man with a red beard; quite probably a man—undescribed—named James Self; possibly a wife or two; avowedly a harried playwright-director. Which had nothing to do with the case. A man may be hated by hundreds and die, quite by accident, under a ten-ton truck. Or, as is always more likely, quietly in bed. Or, which was more apposite, as the chance target of a madman. In the mind, write "Closed" to the case of Anthony Payne.

Captain William Weigand, at his desk in the squad offices in West Twentieth Street, stamped the word "Closed" across his mind and the telephone rang on his desk. That would be Mullins, Sergeant Aloysius, reporting the results of cooperation with detectives of the Charles Street Station in connection with a suspicious death in a furnished room in Bank Street. (Probably suicide, but one or two things didn't check.) Weigand picked up the receiver and said, "Weigand."

Not Sergeant Mullins. Captain Frank, commanding, Fourth Detective District. Surprised to find Weigand around so early. (Weigand had been at his desk for some forty-five minutes.) In re this Payne kill.

"I thought—" Bill Weigand said.

"Sure. So did I. Only—this character on the roof. Turns out to be an old client. You know Brozy?"

Weigand did not know Brozy. It would do Bill good to get around more. Bill didn't doubt it. So?

"Ambrose Light," Frank said and Bill Weigand, not unnaturally, said, "What?"

"Sure," Frank said. "Great little jokers his parents were, some Mr. and Mrs. Light. Turn a psychiatrist loose on Brozy and you'd probably come up with something. But—"

Ambrose Light, called Brozy, was a professional hotel thief, making a modest but fairly consistent living by visiting the rooms of hotel guests, preferably in the absence of the guests. A little here and a little there, it turned out to be Brozy, who owned a useful collection of general keys, and a few other instruments of value in his profession.

Brozy had been following his trade the previous evening in the Hotel King Arthur, the location being purely coincidental but the time a matter of selection. Brozy preferred, naturally, to make his little visits when guests would be most likely to be elsewhere, at this hour at dinner. Brozy liked the quiet hour.

This hour had suddenly, and to him inexplicably, ceased to be quiet at a little after eight the previous evening. Brozy had been trying out a key when, clearly in that very street, all hell broke loose. All hell, to Brozy, was most quickly identified with police sirens.

Brozy found a hall window and looked down from it, and had never seen so many cops spilling out of cruise cars. Nothing like that had ever happend to Brozy before. Hotel detectives, yes. Now and then an unfair guest who pretended to be out while actually being in. but the whole lousy force—

"Jeeze," Brozy said, simply, explaining to Detective Foley in the West Fifty-fourth Street Station House, after he had regained the consciousness lost when he had tried to make a run for it, and had run into a fist. "What I thought was what the hell? On account of, I hadn't touched off no alarm."

As he had looked down, he had seen several cops disappear under the marquee of the King Arthur. That had been enough for Brozy, and he had begun an ascent, by fire stairway. He had been on the third floor when he heard the racket, and the King Arthur was twelve stories high. It was quite a climb for Brozy, whose trade seldom required violent exercise. He went up a final ladder to the roof and made himself inconspicuous in the lee of a parapet.

This had been a mistake, and he freely admitted as much to Detective Foley. If he had got himself into a room and hid out there, under a bed if necessary, he might have got away with it. "I was a nut," Brozy admitted frankly. "How'd I know who you were looking for? Jeeze, Sergeant, I never shot nobody."

"No record of violence," Frank told Bill Weigand. "Just a small-time regular who's been in and out for years. About as likely to kill somebody as—" He paused to consider. "A maiden aunt." He considered again. "Less than some I've met," he added. "Which doesn't prove anything, of course."

"Light heard nothing? Saw nothing?"

"He says not, and I guess he didn't. Matter of fact, I've never seen such an astonished little man. You can't blame him, actually. Oh, we got the wrong man, Bill. Which doesn't prove there wasn't a right man we didn't get, does it?"

Bill agreed it didn't.

"Still a sniper for my money," Frank said.

Bill Weigand said, "Right."

"Only," Frank said, "the old man says for you to get cracking, on your side of the street."

Deputy Chief Inspector Artemus O'Malley, commanding detectives, Borough of Manhattan, had spoken. Bill was mildly surprised he had not heard O'Malley, who after all was only some thirty-four blocks away. He would hear. He would also have to tell O'Malley that the Norths were in it, and listen and say, when opportunity presented, "Yes, chief. Again. I know, chief—"

Sufficient unto the hour.

Bill said, "Right, Johnny," and hung up.

Amost at once the telephone rang again. This was, it appeared, the hour. Bill Weigand picked up the telephone and held the receiver at a suitable distance from his ear. He said, "Weigand" and then, "Oh," and put the earpiece against his ear. He said, "Hello, Pam."

"You didn't sound natural at first," Pam North said.

"I thought you were the inspector," Bill Weigand said, and it was Pam's turn to say, in a most understanding fashion, "Oh." Then she said that something had happened that she thought he ought to know about.

"Pipeline," Pam said. "Or should it be listening post?"

"I don't know," Bill said. "What, Pamela?"

"Me. Being used as. To you, of course. It's happened before, you know."

"Right," Bill said. "What's happened before, Pam?"

"People come to us to find out what you're up to," Pam said. "Are you sure you're all right, Bill? First you thought I was O'Malley. Do I sound like O'Malley?"

"No. Who wants to find out through you what I am, as you put it, up to?"

"Mrs. Payne. The Widow Payne. Only that wasn't all of it, I don't think. I think she's afraid she's let some cat out of some bag. *Stilts! Quit that!* Scratching a sofa. Where was I?"

"Cat out of bag," Bill said.

"Of course. Listen—"

Bill listened. When Pam had finished he asked questions. She was sure that Lauren Payne had not said, to her, anything that revealed anything? Pam could remember nothing. Sure that she had called Blaine Smythe a friend of her husband's, not of hers? Yes, and Pam didn't believe it for a minute. Bill should have seen them—

"Right," Bill Weigand said. "I don't doubt you're right."

Nor, knowing Pam, did he doubt. Pamela North has now and again put two and two together and come up with odd sums, but two was each time two, and only the addition wrong.

The woman who, after the doctor had given sedation, had stayed with Lauren Payne?

"A housekeeper. Or assistant housekeeper. She thought her name was Mason. Something like Mason. Why?"

"If I," Bill said, "were afraid I'd let a cat out of a bag, I'd look everywhere the cat might have gone, wouldn't you? If I was afraid I'd talked out of turn—"

"Of *course,*" Pam said. "I should have—" She paused. "Never mind," she said.

"You left her with the impression that we still think it's—what the *News* this morning called 'Mad Killer'?"

"I tried to. I don't know why, exactly. Or whether it worked exactly. Do you?"

"It's still probable," Bill said. "Only, the boys uptown thought they had the man and didn't. Not the man. Only Brozy." He told her, briefly, about Brozy.

"The poor man," Pam said. "So like Eve, in a way."

Bill merely waited.

"You pick an apple," Pam said, "and the heavens fall. Ambrose must have felt that. So much commotion about such a little thing. What else, Bill?"

Lieutenant John Stein opened the door of Bill's office. He widened his brown eyes. He pointed upward and shook the pointing hand.

"Sorry, Pam," Bill said. "The inspector's trying to

get me." He hung up. He remembered he had forgotten to tell Pam not to get herself in trouble, as she always did, as Jerry always did. Usually to no avail. He took the telephone up. He said, "Put the chief on, please," and held the receiver well away from his ear. He listened for a time. He said, "Yes, Inspector, I'm afraid so. Again."

6

Pamela had expected to have lunch at home, alone, contesting with cats for morsels. She had not, certainly, expected to lunch at Sardi's and not only at Sardi's, but with Alice Draycroft. She had, on the telephone, said, "Well, I don't know whether—" and Alice had said, *"Darling!* It's been years and years. Seeing you yesterday made me *realize."*

It was not entirely clear what, with such impact, Alice Draycroft had realized. Certainly not that, since school—umpteen years ago, Pam thought, putting the telephone back in its cradle—she and Pam had met only now and then, as an actress, usually with a part, may meet the wife of a publisher. Even in school they had not been close. Alice had been ahead of Pam in school; Alice had been a star in productions of the Dramatic Club and once, once only, Pam had played a maid with a duster. (And a few lines of background comment on the people she dusted for.) It was not an adequate basis for a lifelong friendship. Not that Alice, met now and then, wasn't fun. I'm a pushover, Pam thought, and changed from the gray-blue dress to another—blue-gray—more suitable for Sardi's. She decided that Sardi's justified her mink stole.

"Darling!" Alice said, at only a little after one. (Pam had waited hardly ten minutes.) "So *wonderful* you could. Henri, darling."

Henri darling (Henry Perkins at home) said, "Ah, Miss Draycroft. If you will, please?" They would, please. The table was in a corner. "A stinger, darling?" Alice said.

"Martini," Pam said. "Please."

"So *brave* of you," Alice said. "Martinis always—"

"Very cold, very dry, lemon peel," Pam said, taking no chances, even at Sardi's.

"And a bloody mary," Alice said. "Wasn't this a wonderful idea of mine?"

In fact, it began to seem a very pleasant, if not entirely wonderful, idea. It had to be said—it was gladly thought—of Alice Draycroft that she lifted you up. Sometimes, afterward, you were a little tired, but up you had been. Pam, more the Algonquin type, went seldom to Sardi's, and change is pleasant.

"Wonderful," Pam said. "Such a nice place to visit."

"Darling," Alice said. "You're wonderful, darling. And how's Jerry?"

Pam said Jerry was fine, curbing a slight inclination to say that he was *"wonderful."* She knew she should continue; should ask about the condition of Alice's husband. She was almost sure that Alice had a husband; Alice almost always did have. But, "How's yours?" seemed hardly a graceful query.

"Betwixt and between, darling," Alice said. She had always been quick on the uptake, Alice; she never embarrassed without cause. "Such a lovely party you and Jerry gave for everybody."

"Well," Pam said.

"Up to a point of course," Alice said. "Do you still see that wonderful policeman of yours? Such a lamb, I thought he was."

Pam checked her memory quickly, seeking the opportunity obviously at some time presented Alice Draycroft to discover lamb-like qualities in Captain William Weigand. It came back—the four of them, she and Jerry, Bill and Dorian, at dinner somewhere. Celebrating something? Because "21" came to mind as the somewhere. And Alice, at first across the room, saying "Pam *darling*" and then with a man—a current husband—briefly at their table.

"Yes," Pam said. "You mean Bill Weigand, don't you? Quite often, as a matter of fact."

"I suppose," Alice said, "he's up to his *ears* now about poor Mr. Payne."

So that, Pam thought, was that. The inside of things was as precious to Alice Draycroft as to John Gunther. This was part of an innocence which was, probably far more than she herself suspected, part of Alice. "I oughtn't to tell you who told me, but the real truth is—" Nevertheless, in all innocence. This time, "I happen to know the police think—" But without pretension, in all innocence.

"I suppose so," Pam said and, before Alice uttered a diminished "Oh," thought herself unkind. "I thought, since it was Jerry's party it happened at—" Alice said, hope dying slowly.

"They think probably it was just a crazy person with a gun," Pam said. She considered; there would hardly be any secrecy about Brozy. "They caught one," Pam said, "but they're having to throw him back, Bill says. A hotel thief named—"

She told Alice Draycroft, who was understandably delighted with his name, about Ambrose Light.

"He must have felt he'd hit the jackpot without even pulling the lever," Alice said. "The poor darling. But they still think it was somebody like that? I mean—" She let it hang, looked beyond Pam. Her expressive face expressed delight. She said, projecting, *"Faith*. Faith *darling*. We're over here."

For the second time within less than twenty-four hours, Pam was surprised when she looked at Faith Constable, walking toward them—shimmering toward them. At the center of her surprise was the conviction that Faith Constable should be bigger. On stage she was, somehow, never small—rather, she seemed to be any height she chose to be, needed to be. But she was, coming now between tables at Sardi's, surely not more than five feet tall and she moved as if she weighed nothing whatever. And, it was preposterous for her to be the age she so obviously had to be.

There was a second reason, a quite different reason, for Pamela North's surprise. It was that Faith Constable, onetime wife of the late Anthony Payne, was not herself at all surprised, but shimmered toward them precisely as if she had expected to find both of them there, waiting, at a corner table at Sardi's. Pam looked quickly at Alice Draycroft, who looked back with surpassing innocence. "Isn't this *nice,* darling?" Alice said. "The nicest things just happen, I always think."

Chance met at Sardi's. How actors love to act, Pam thought. How much more likely things are to happen if properly nudged. Why?

Pam had indeed met Faith Constable. Of course Faith remembered Pamela North. There was indeed room at the table for a third; Henri (darling) would see that the daiquiri was very dry.

"We were talking about poor Tony, darling," Alice

Draycroft said, and Faith continued to look entirely unsurprised. She nodded her head.

"Who isn't?" she said. "He'd be so pleased. Under other circumstances, of course. Or shouldn't I say that?"

The question appeared to be directed to Pam North, who could think of no answer better than a smile and a slight lifting of the shoulders.

"The police still think it was what they call a sniper," Alice said, bringing her chance-met friend up to date. "They got one but he wasn't right, darling. He was named Ambrose Light."

Faith Constable smiled in a slightly abstracted fashion.

"Ambrose Light*ship,* darling," Alice said, and Faith nodded mild appreciation, and seemed to remain at some distance. The daiquiri came. She sipped it, and looked over it at Pam.

"We're not taking you in, are we, Mrs. North?" Faith said. "I asked Alice to arrange this. But you already knew that, didn't you?"

"Well," Pam said, "you didn't seem astonished to find us here."

And she was again surprised. On stage, Faith Constable was notably oblique. "Mrs. Constable's attack is never frontal," one critic had written, rather recently. "This is one of the charms of her highly individual method. All effects are, as it were, outflanked. As a result even what should have been evident often comes as a surprise to delight the mind." It appeared that Faith Constable, offstage, had other methods.

"Mrs. North," Faith said, "I know that you and your husband sometimes"—she hesitated momentarily for a word—"help the police. Everybody knows that."

She ought to say that to Deputy Chief Inspector Artemus O'Malley, Pam thought briefly. He'd tell her a thing or two. On the other hand—

"It's—just happened," Pam said. "Only because once a long time ago we found somebody in a bathtub." She considered the structure of her explanation. "Somebody's dead body," Pam said. "So we met Bill Weigand and—" She felt herself drifting. "All right," Pam North said. "And what, Mrs. Constable?"

But she was quite certain she knew what. "Occupation: Conduit." She would put that down next time, instead of "Housewife." Or, perhaps, "Go-between."

"If you want to know what the police think," Pam said, "shouldn't you ask the police? If—"

"Mrs. North," Faith said, "please don't be cross with me."

She said this very simply, as one might ask a favor. She looked at Pam steadily, and there was simplicity in the way she looked at Pam. Pam was sure it was— Of course, she was an actess and—

"I'm sorry," Pam said. "I'm not cross. I don't really know what the police think. Bill—that's Captain Weigand—" Faith nodded her head. "Says that probably it was only a sniper. That your—that Mr. Payne—was a target. Not anything more. But—"

"My former husband," Faith Constable said, "had an ability to get himself disliked. I know that. I ought to know. I learned, very rapidly, to dislike him heartily. Mrs. North, Willings is a great writer."

People of the theater use the word "great" with easy familiarity. But Faith, using it in this connection, used it as if she meant it. It was not, however, entirely clear what she meant by it.

"I don't know him," she said. "Oh—I've met him. That isn't it." She smiled suddenly, and the smile changed her face, brought the shimmer back to her. "Kids want autographs," she said. "They wriggle and titter and go eek! and they're rather a nuisance and, sometimes, rather sweet. I'd like to be a kid and wriggle and titter and say, 'Please, Mr. Willings?' " She paused and the smile changed. "Not really," she said. "A way of putting it. They'll suspect him, won't they? Because of this childish brawl. And—the indignity."

"Perhaps," Pam said. "I don't—"

"He's too important to be—damaged," Faith said. "Even if—" She stopped; very obviously, she stopped herself, abruptly, on check-rein.

"If you mean," Pam said, and now she was direct, as simply direct, as Faith Constable had unexpectedly become, "even if he killed Mr. Payne—no, Mrs. Constable. There aren't that kind of exceptions."

Faith Constable was shaking her head seconds before Pam finished. But she let Pam finish.

"I didn't mean that," she said, then. "Something quite different. It's—" She stopped again, but this time, Pam thought, for her mind to choose the words it wanted. "If Willings did kill Tony," she said, "there's nothing to be done about it. It'll be tragic, but there'll be nothing to be done about it. Tony's as well dead— oh, nobody's as well dead, I shouldn't say that—Tony wasn't really much of anybody, and Willings may write a dozen books, and everybody'll gain by them. *Every*body."

It didn't matter if she overstated, Pam thought. And people had worshiped at lesser shrines.

"That doesn't matter," Faith said. "I realize that. If Willings killed him—but I don't think he did. I think I know who may have and—"

It had happened before, and Pam had grown rather

tired of it. For all her growing sympathy for—call it empathy with—Faith Constable, Pam felt irritation stirring. If people had things to tell the police—

"Please," Faith said. It occurred to Pam that her own face, also, probably was expressive. "Yes, there is something I want the police to hear about. It may be nothing. They may already know. And, it's quite true I don't want to go to them." She watched Pam's face; evidently saw something in it almost before Pam had herself caught up.

"Part of it's the bad publicity," Faith said. "I don't deny it. I don't want 'Actress Grilled in Ex-Husband's Murder.' Or however they'd put it. I don't want that at all. That's cowardly selfish, so all right it's cowardly selfish. And if I have to, in the end, all right, I have to in the end. But—there's more. I—"

"Listen, darlings," Alice Draycroft said. "Do we have another drink? Or do we have lunch? Or—what I mean is, darlings, how's to take five?"

Faith Constable looked at her friend, and fellow actress, somewhat as if she had never seen her before. After a moment, she smiled a little vaguely, as if she had come back from a great distance to surroundings only a little familiar, and said, "All right, dear. Perhaps we should." Alice Draycroft looked over her shoulder and a waiter said, "Yes, Miss Draycroft?" and she made a circling movement with the index finger of her right hand. The waiter said, "Yes, Miss Draycroft," and went. Faith, very carefully, fitted a cigarette into a holder; very carefully lighted the cigarette and sat, looking at the lighter flame for seconds before she snapped the lighter shut. It occurred to Pam that she was looking, not at the tiny flame, but far back to where she had been, been brought back from. The waiter came with drinks. Faith sipped from her glass, and did not look at either of the others—looked at nothing.

"I was very young twenty-five years ago—no, it was twenty-six," Faith said and only after she had said that looked at Pam North again. "The story of my life," she said. "More than you'd asked for. Not all of it." She smiled at Pam, and there was a certain apology in her smile. "I was younger than I should have been, of course. I wasn't really so very young. Not as years go."

She paused again. After a moment, as abruptly as before, she began again.

"I was just realizing," she said, "that I wasn't going to be a writer. I'd wanted very much to be a writer, and not nearly so much to act. But it turned out I could act and couldn't write. I suppose that's why I've always been a little that way—a little hipped—about writers. I suppose that was why I married him in the first place." She paused again. The pausing—between ideas, now and then between words, was, Pam thought, a part of artistry, of a craft which had, in turn, become part of Faith Constable. "I'm talking about Tony," Faith said. "He was a real writer—anyway, he thought he was, persuaded me he was.

"We were only married a couple of years," she said. "I've always said that I was the one who decided to call it quits. That was true. But—only partly true. He wasn't a very nice person, poor Tony. I wasn't nearly so young after a year of it—old enough to notice how very un-nice he was. But that wasn't all." Once more she paused. She took a breath. (How many times, Pam thought, must she, on stage, have drawn breath in so, miming hesitancy before action. And—how much truth there was in it, method or no method.)

"He walked out first," Faith said. "I hated to admit

it then, and I don't like to now. He found another girl—a younger girl. Oh, ten years younger. A girl who appreciated him more. He always needed so much appreciation, poor Tony. A girl named Gladdis Arn—spelled it g-l-a-d-d-i-s, the poor thing. Well—" And once more she paused. "There is a point to this," she said and seemed, for the first time in some minutes, to realize Pam as an audience, and as a person. "I'll come to the point of it."

She sipped from her glass, but the glass remained, still, almost full.

"I went to Reno," she said. "As soon as he could, Tony married Gladdis Arn. She was—I don't quite know how to say it—just a pretty girl. Pretty, full of admiration and, I'm afraid, not very bright. Tony divorced her after about a year—divorced her and said the child she'd just had wasn't his and made the court believe it. Another man helped—a man, Gladdis said, she'd met only once, only casually. The man said it had been different—very different. I always thought he was lying, always thought Tony had hired him. Tony had begun to make money by then."

She crushed out the cigarette, which had burned down to the rim of the holder.

"Part of it," she said, "he made out of me, in a way. I was a character in a book he wrote. Very, very bitchy, I was in the book. It didn't sell very well, but the movies bought it and Tony—I've met a good many heels, but it's sometimes hard to believe in Tony—suggested they might get me to play the bitch." Suddenly, she chuckled. "Sometimes," she said, "you had almost to admire the bastard. Anyway—"

Anyway, Anthony Payne got rid (legally unless proved otherwise, and it had not been) of a girl who hadn't, after all, appreciated him quite enough and of her child—a boy of about a month. He also, of course, freed himself from any legal need to support Gladdis, now Gladdis Arn again.

"So far as I know," Faith said, "he never did anything for her and—"

"You may as well," Alice Draycroft said, "admit you kept her going, darling. We won't tell anybody."

"Sometimes—" Faith Constable said, darkly, "you—" She did not finish. "That hasn't anything to do with anything." Alice started to speak again. "You talk too much, darling," Faith told her, and Alice shrugged her shoulders. She looked at Pam and spread expressive hands in a gesture of hopelessness.

Gladdis Arn had married again some three years after the divorce, and after that Faith had not seen much of her and, finally, nothing at all of her. She could not remember, now, the name of Gladdis's second husband, although she had known it once. She had heard that the son, whose right to any name was legally questionable, had taken that of his stepfather. The second husband, whatever his name had been, had died about four years after he had married Gladdis. Faith had heard that, anyway. And Gladdis had disappeared until—

"Yesterday," Faith said. "During the party. A strictly terrible woman in the damnedest dress—"

"Not," Pam North said, "a pink chiffon dress?"

Faith blinked her eyes at Pam. She said, "Clairvoyant?"

"No," Pam said. "I had the experience."

"Anyway, I took it for a while and then I said, very ladylike, 'I'm afraid you'll have to excuse me, darling. I've got to go to the john.'" Faith appeared momentarily diverted. She chuckled softly and said that they should have seen the poor thing's face. They would have thought she had never heard of anyone's going to the john.

"Only," Faith said, "then I did have to go somewhere, so I thought, since I was going on afterward, I might as well actually. And I was going down the corridor to it and—and there she was. Gladdis."

Gladdis had been wearing a white dress, which had the look of a uniform. A ring of keys was clipped to the belt of the dress, and she was standing, with a maid, in front of a linen closet, and pointing into the closet and, clearly, explaining something to the maid.

"She stepped back when I came along," Faith said, "to give me room. And faced me—and her face turned blank. Eyes blank, whole face blank. She said, 'Excuse me, miss,' in a blank voice. It was—" She paused. "She had never seen me before," she said. "She was acting it, y'know. Overacting it, the poor thing. So—well, that was the way she wanted it and I—oh, I suppose I smiled to show I'd heard her, and I went on to the john. But—it was Gladdis."

"You're sure?" Pam said. "After so many years and—"

"Yes," Faith said, "I'm quite sure. Oh—she's changed. We all change. But, I had some reason to remember her, y'know. A reason that once had seemed a very good one. It was Gladdis. Apparently she's a housekeeper of some sort. Not just a maid but—she works at the hotel. She was there yesterday, while the party was going on. And—she would have heard about this ruckus between Tony and Willings, wouldn't she? It would have spread all over. And—"

She paused and lighted another cigarette.

"The poor thing had more reason than anybody to hate Tony Payne," Faith said, and spoke slowly. "To her, more than to anybody else, he had been the heel of all time. And with Willings set up as—"

She looked at her watch and shook her head over what she saw. She flipped the cigarette out of the holder and ground it out, and pushed her chair back a little. But, once more, she paused.

"The boy," she said. "He'd be in his early twenties now, wouldn't he? And—with as much cause to hate as his mother. More—the young can hate so much more. Whether Tony was really his father or wasn't—" She did not finish that. She moved her chair a little farther from the table.

"You can see," she said to Pam. "I hope you can— why I don't want to be the one to—to go to the police. I suppose telling you, leaving it up to you, is—well, pretty much the same thing. But, it doesn't seem quite so bitchy. Maybe I really mean that it won't *look* quite so bitchy. I suppose it's because of the goldfish bowl I live in and—people, all the darlings who love me—" She broke off. "Not you, Alice," she said. "They'd all say, 'Took Faith Constable long enough, but she got her own back. A bit of a bitch, Faith Constable, but what would you expect?'"

She stood up, now. Alice looked up at her, and she shook her head.

"Rehearsal," she said. "Lars will be frothing already. Forgive me, darlings. Have a nice lunch."

She started to shimmer away. But she stopped, turned back.

"I remember," she said. "Mason. That was the name of the man she married. Mason."

And then she went.

7

Deputy Chief Inspector Artemus O'Malley had, on the whole, taken it rather well. A few screams which somewhat resembled prayers; a few shouted warnings about listening to people nobody could make head or tail of; some violent instructions that Weigand remember *he* was the cop, and not that couple of screwy amateurs and particularly the dame. But no order to come, forthwith, to O'Malley's office in West Fifty-fourth Street; no direct threat that, if he caught the Norths messing around it, he would, "g.d. it to hell," toss them in the tank and throw away the key.

Bill Weigand could not remember that the inspector had ever, before, been so moderate on an issue which was, to him, immoderate. The inspector was, conceivably, softening up. Or, perhaps, he was merely getting tired. He had fought the battle of the Norths for a very long time, but not to much avail. It was his conviction that the Norths loused things up; that any case in which they were involved became improperly complicated and that this was clearly the fault of the Norths. He felt, also, that, with the Norths present, Weigand forgot the duty of a cop: Keep it simple and arrest the most likely. In this case, a sniper, by preference, but—

"About this Willings guy," Inspector O'Malley had said when he turned from the Norths. "This Payne guy knocks him down in front of a lot of people and from what I hear this Willings guy goes around banging himself on the chest, like this Tarzan guy. Lick any man in the bar, that's what I hear Willings is. So what's the matter with the Willings guy, Bill?"

"Nothing," Bill said. "I don't say you're not right, chief. Only, we don't want to rush things, do we? He's a fairly important man—"

"Important? Whatja mean important? Way I get it, he's just a writer. Book writer."

"Well—"

"That's what I mean," O'Malley said. "This North guy gets into it, and you get screwy ideas. Like a book writer's being an important guy. On account, this North guy publishes books. You see what I mean, Bill?"

"Right. Only—"

"A guy writes for newspapers," O'Malley said, "and I don't say you wouldn't have something. Or even magazines. But this guy just writes books."

"Right. I remember that, chief."

"You young cops," O'Malley said, tolerantly. "Got anything for the newspaper boys?"

"Nothing they need to have. Anyway, they ought to be happy for now."

"There's the afternoons, Bill."

"Give 'em Brozy, chief. They'll like Brozy."

"They'll kid us," O'Malley said. "But, O.K., Bill. So—wait a minute. Listen, Bill. Are there any cats in this one?" There was entreaty in his tone.

85

"Not that I know of."

"Thank God," O'Malley said, and hung up.

Bill went out to the squad room. Sergeant Mullins was at his desk, and a head motion summoned him.

"Bank Street's a suicide, O.K.," Mullins reported. "Girl trouble. Wrote a note and mailed it to the girl."

"Thoughtful of him," Bill said. "On this Payne kill, Sergeant. Mrs. Payne went around to see Mrs. North this morning and—"

"Oh," Mullins said, "another one of those, Loot?" He also sighed deeply.

"And," Bill repeated, having for the time had enough of that, "apparently—possibly, anyway—is worried whether she said something she shouldn't. When Mrs. North told her her husband was dead. After that, there was a woman with her—just sitting with her, I suppose—for a time. A housekeeper, works for the hotel. Name of Mason. Mrs. Payne didn't say anything that sounded out of the way to Mrs. North. But it could be that to this housekeeper—"

"O.K., Loot-I-mean-Captain," Mullins said. "We go—"

"You," Bill said. "Right?"

Mullins said "Sure." He went. . . .

The bookstore seemed, somehow, to be in hiding. It was on an inconspicuous street in the Village, far from the strange life of Eighth Street. It was three steps below street level, as if it flinched from public view. The lettering on the window glass was at the bottom, and small, and said: "James Self, Books." Weigand went down into the area and opened the bookshop door and, from some distance, a small bell tinkled. For the moment, nothing else happened.

There were shelves of books on either side of the narrow shop. There were two easy chairs with their backs to the street windows; there was a table beside each chair, and on each table a spray of cigarettes in a pewter container. A long table ran down the center of the room, and there were books on it in varicolored jackets. Waiting, Bill Weigand looked at the books. A small stack of Gardner Willings's latest. Several titles in French. Two titles by Marquand. Cozzens was represented; Anthony Payne was not. There were light footsteps from a rear room and a girl with dark hair and large dark eyes, with a singularly white skin, came out of it. She wore a loose sweater and a tweed skirt and loafers.

She said, in a somewhat faraway voice, and in a soft voice, "Can I help you? Or would you prefer to browse?"

It occurred to Bill Weigand that the words had been learned by rote; had been planned, whether by the girl or someone else, as a conventional expression of a detached, noncommercial attitude. Certainly the pretty girl spoke as if she were weary of the words. She spoke entirely without animation.

And yet, as she had come into the room, there had been animation in her young body. Much can, Bill Weigand believes, be told about people by the way they move. (He sometimes wonders whether it was not extraordinary grace of movement of which he was first conscious when he looked, long since, at a girl named Dorian. But he can no longer think of Dorian Weigand in segments.)

This dark girl moved freshly, muscles quick in supple body. Only her voice was tired, indifferent, as if her mind went slowly through its motions.

Weigand wondered if he could see Mr. Self. In the same tone of detachment, of indifference, she said that she was afraid Mr. Self was out. But if there was some particular book? If an especially rare book he would, indeed, have to see Mr. Self. But—if, perhaps, he wanted them to search for a book? She could make a note of what he wanted—

"No," Bill said. "Nothing like that, miss—"

He gave her opportunity. She did not seem to hear him.

"I wonder," he said, "if you've got Payne's new one in stock yet? Anthony Payne? *The Liberators,* I think it's called. Out yest—"

He stopped because the girl had drawn back. It seemed to him that her dark eyes widened; that the tiny muscles around them set. Her skin had been white, but with glow under it. Suddenly her face was flatly white.

"What do you want?" she said. Her voice did not increase in volume; it was still a soft voice. But its whole timbre was very different.

"What?" he said. "Why, Anthony Payne's new—"

"No," she said. "You brought his name up, didn't you. To see what—what I'd do?"

And that, of course, was true enough. There might be one very pretty, dark-haired, dark-eyed, girl in James Self's shop and another in his life—one (what had Willings said?) "tender" girl. It had seemed worthwhile finding out. He had, he thought, found out.

Candy from a baby, Bill thought. A singularly defenseless baby.

"Who are you?" the girl said. And then, unexpectedly, "I suppose, whoever you are, you're very proud of yourself."

Bill found that he wasn't, particularly. Policemen have to take candy from those who have it. The girl wasn't, certainly, stupid. Merely—innocent? Merely "tender"?

"Right," Bill said. "I'm a detective. And—"

"What do you want to see Jim about?" The voice was a little higher now.

Bill managed, he hoped, to look surprised; even to look blank.

"Why," he said, "Payne's killing, miss." He tried to get surprise into his voice—surprise that she had missed the obvious. (Mullins can do this better, Bill thought.) "Not Mr. Self more than anybody else. We're trying to see everybody who was at this—" he hesitated—"press party, I guess they call it. See if anybody can tell us anything to help." He smiled at the pretty girl, and thought some warmth came back under her very white skin. "Just one of dozens, I am," Bill said. "Were you at this party yourself, miss?"

Muscles around eyes had relaxed. Fine. Taking candy from a baby. All right—fine.

"I?" she said. "Good heavens no. I was minding the store. That's what Mr. Self pays me for."

"Sure," Bill said. "Can't leave any avenue unexplored, as the regulations say." (Mr. Self, now. Jim a moment ago. Baby trying to get her candy back.) "You expect Mr. Self soon?"

"Oh yes," she said. "It shouldn't be—" And stopped abruptly. "He did," she said, "say something about going to an auction. I'd forgotten that. If he did—heaven knows."

Bill Weigand sighed—a tired cop, doing the dull things he was told to do.

"He was at this party, though?" Bill said. "Somehow I got the idea it was for—oh, book reviewers. People like that." Not owners of unimportant bookshops, his tone implied. (He hoped.)

"Oh," she said, "Mr. Self is a critic too. Quite an important one where—where it's important." How does one explain these things to a dumb policeman?

her tone asked. "And he's starting a magazine. A magazine of—" She looked at Bill, and shook her pretty head. Looking for a word within my scope, Bill thought. "Comment," the girl said. "Literary comment. About books that really matter. Not just—"

She made a graceful gesture toward the bright-jacketed books on the long table. Her gesture seemed to dismiss them—Cozzens and Marquand and all.

"Of course," she said, "we have to handle—well, everything here. Best sellers and everything." It was a little, Bill thought, as if she were saying that cockroaches get in everywhere. "Some of our customers want things like that," she said.

Animated enough, now. Trotting along gayly, now, on the hobbyhorse of enthusiasm.

"Most of them," she said, "are—well, different."

"Writers, I suppose," Bill said, trying to remember how Mullins would say it, and speak accordingly. "People like this—what's his name? Williams?"

"If you mean Tennessee Williams," she said. "I don't think—he lives in Key West, you know."

"Thinking of somebody else," Bill said. "Doesn't matter. I'd better be getting—" He started to turn. He said, "Wait a minute. Willings. That's the one I was thinking of. Writers like that. Or, for that matter, Anthony Payne."

"Not Will—" she said, and stopped, and the little muscles about her large, and for that matter very beautiful, dark eyes once more tightened.

"But," Bill Weigand said, "Payne. Often, miss—? I think you'd better tell me your name."

She hesitated for a moment. She said, "Why?" He merely waited. When she spoke, her voice was flat again.

"Rhodes," she said. "Jo-An Rhodes."

"Miss Rhodes," Bill said, "you saw Mr. Payne

away from the shop, didn't you? Went to dinner with him? Things like—"

"You haven't any—"

"Yes," Bill said. "To ask. Because we have to find out everything about Mr. Payne we can find out—who he knew, who he saw. Yes, even who he took to dinner. If you've some reason not to answer—"

She was shaking her head, by then. She said, "You'll misunderstand. Try to make something out of it." Very young; a little frightened.

"No," Bill said. "Nothing that isn't there. You did see him? Often?"

"Several times. It was—there wasn't anything. To dinner a few times and—oh, to the theater. And once up to have dinner at a place in the country. I can go where I want to. With—with people I want—"

"Of course," Bill said. "I don't question that. But, Miss Rhodes, *did Mr. Self?*"

She looked surprised—managed to look surprised. That was it, Bill thought—"managed." Candy from—

"Mr. Self?" she repeated, and got surprise into her soft voice. "Why on earth should— Oh, I see what you mean. It was always after I was through here, of course. I only work until—"

"No," Bill said. "That wasn't what I meant, Miss Rhodes. You know it wasn't, don't you? Because— how do you want me to put it? Mr. Self doesn't want you going with other men? Particularly men such as Mr. Payne apparently was? And, of course, married men and—"

"His wife didn't—" Again she did not finish.

"Understand him?" Bill said, in a certain tone, and at that she shook her head from side to side.

"Care," she said. "It was—their marriage was just a—formality. It isn't as if—"

"He told you that?"

91

She saw it; saw it too late. If it had all been as casual as she said, Payne wouldn't have—oh, she saw it. But at that moment, a little bell tinkled in the room behind the shop.

She was facing toward the front of the shop. She spoke as Bill Weigand turned to face the door.

"Jim," she said. "This man's a detective. He's been—"

"Good afternoon, Mr. Self," Bill said. "My name's Weigand. From—"

"Captain," Self said. He was a tall, spare man in his early thirties. He had black hair, which was beginning a little to recede. He had a wide forehead and a wide mouth and a surprisingly square jaw. "Homicide, Manhattan West. Badgering children, Captain?"

"I'm not a—" Jo-An said, and her voice was not indifferent now. There was indignation in the young voice.

"Of course you are, Jo-Jo," James Self said. "I'm sure the captain discovered that. Get what you were after, Weigand?"

"Oh," Bill said, "I was just waiting around until you got back, Mr. Self. To see whether you'd noticed anything at the party which might help us. There's a lot of rou—"

"The hell with that," Self said. "Jo-Jo—dust some books, will you? Or read one. Or, twiddle your pretty thumbs."

"I don't have—" the girl said and Self said, "Sh-h-h." He said, "You want to see me, come on," and walked toward the rear of the shop. "The insufferable—" the girl said, and gave it up. Bill Weigand followed the spare man who, he now realized, vaguely reminded him of somebody he had met before. In almost the same moment, he remembered who—a lineman for a light and power company; a man called Harry; a very tough young man indeed and, certainly, no frequenter of bookshops. Bill was faintly amused by the vagary of his own mind.

The room immediately in the rear of the shop was small, dim, obviously a storeroom. Beyond it, the room Weigand followed James Self into was as obviously an office. It had a tall window giving on a garden. There was a desk, rather cluttered. Self sat at the desk, back to window, and motioned, the gesture quick, peremptory, toward a chair. Bill thought, the image of Harry, and sat down.

"What did you get out of the child?" Self said, and his voice, too, was peremptory.

"You seem," Bill said, mildly, "to think there was something to get, Mr. Self."

He was asked if he wanted to kid around.

"Very well," Bill said. "That she was seeing a good deal of Anthony Payne, a man who's got himself killed. A good deal more than you approved of, I think. How strong was your disapproval, Mr. Self?"

"So," Self said, "that's your line, is it? No demented sniper, anymore?"

"I haven't a line yet," Bill said. "I'm looking for a line. Well?"

"She's a baby," Self said. "You can see that, can't you? Pretty, bright enough. Hipped on what she used to call the 'literary life.' " His wide mouth twisted itself into a smile—a rather unexpected smile, somehow at odds with his manner, with the aggressive squareness of his jaw. "Cured her of the expression. Not, I'm afraid, of the attitude. Fair game for a man like Payne. Distinguished man of letters." He made a sound of utter contempt. "She's a little goose—pretty, downy little goose." He seemed to speak with anger.

Bill waited.

"He was a stinker," Self said. "What you ought to be looking for is somebody to pin a medal on."

"Perhaps," Bill said. "But we're not hired for that. I take it you felt strongly about this? Miss Rhodes seeing Payne? Going about with—"

"Who wouldn't? Except another stinker like Payne?"

"You seem to feel responsible for her," Bill said. "Why?"

"Nobody's responsible for anybody," Self said. "You see a kid fall into a sewer, you try to pull it out, if you happen to be on hand. Sure, I disapproved. I disapprove of all the bad things that happen to everybody. Take it that I'm against sin."

Bill Weigand smiled faintly, and moved his head slowly from side to side.

"All right," James Self said, "she's a lovely little thing. I'm sitting here in this cave, growling, and one day she walks in and says she's come from Chicago because life there is sterile—whatever the hell she meant by that—and can I give her a job? Because she wants to be some place that has something to do with books." He shook his own head. "Good God," he said.

Bill kept on waiting.

"So—" Self said. "She lighted up the cave. And I did need somebody to tell people please to feel free to browse. She tell you that?"

Bill nodded.

"Her father manufactures buttons," Self said. "Gives you pause, doesn't it? Until you remember buttons have to come from somewhere. And that somebody must make—oh, rubber bands. Paper clips. Hairpins, for God's sake. Bit button man. And her mother—what the hell am I going into all this for?" He looked hard at Weigand. "You think I fell for her," he said. "Was overcome by yen."

"Well—"

"Not that," Self said. "I don't say nothing like that. But not flatly that. She's—what the hell's the use? Keep it simple. That's what you want, isn't it? Payne grabs off my girl and I kill Payne. Only—she isn't my girl. And I didn't kill Payne."

"Right," Bill said. "Whatever you say."

"Until you can prove different," Self said.

"Unless I can."

"How did you get onto this—angle? Or is that none of my business?"

"Payne brought Miss Rhodes into a restaurant," Bill said. "You saw them. Seemed angry—upset."

"Willings," Self said, "is a blabbermouth. Has to put everything into words. Has to listen to his own words. Try them out. Regardless—" Self broke off and leaned back in his chair. "And God," he said, "how the bastard can write!" He leaned forward again.

"And where was I at the time of the crime? And who was with me? And have I got a revolver—"

"Rifle," Bill said. "Twenty-two target. Probably with a telescopic sight."

"I said revolver just to throw you off," Self said. "Sure I knew it was a rifle."

Bill sighed, audibly.

"No," Self said. "Revolver or rifle or popgun. No. I left this damn party—"

"By the way. How'd you happen to go to the party?"

"Got invited. Thought there might be a performance. Couldn't see Willings passing up a chance like that. Not after Payne's review."

"You saw the performance?"

"Saw it. Thought it only fair. Contrived unhappy

95

ending. Good guy felled by bad guy. You've considered Willings? Unexpectedly deflated. Made an ass out of, to put it simply. Which he wouldn't like at all."

"Yes. You went alone to the party?"

"You mean, did I take Jo-Jo? No. After the show was over I came back here. Upstairs, that is. I've got an apartment upstairs. Which Miss Jo-An Rhodes does not share. That's for the record. I read a while and had a drink and about nine o'clock I got hungry and went out and got some food. That I could prove, I suppose. Not the rest of it. Well?"

That, Weigand told him, about did it. For the moment. Bill went, alone, through the small storeroom and into the shop. Jo-An Rhodes was sitting in one of the chairs, back to window, reading. She looked up as he came into the room; looked up quickly.

Since the light was behind her, Bill Weigand could not see her face clearly. There was no real explanation, therefore, for the sudden conviction in his mind that the girl—the very pretty girl—was frightened. She looked at him as he walked the length of the room, and did not speak. She did not turn her head after he had passed her, nor as he went out through the door, while a distant bell tinkled his departure. So he could not, still, see her face clearly enough to read anything in it. Nothing to go on, really. All the same, he thought her frightened.

In the area outside, he turned and looked back into the shop. Jo-An Rhodes was going toward the rear of the shop. She was going so quickly that she seemed almost to be running.

8

Mrs. Gladys Mason was, certainly, employed by the Hotel Dumont. She was one of six assistant housekeepers. She lived in the hotel—in Room 1701A. She would now—the assistant manager looked at his watch. Since it was after one o'clock, she would be on duty. Certainly he would be glad to arrange for Sergeant Mullins to talk to her. Couldn't imagine Mrs. Mason—seemed a good, reliable person—would know anything about "this tragic event." (The assistant manager spoke of the tragedy of the event with deep sincerity. The Hotel Dumont didn't like any part of it—or not, at any rate, the last part of it. The scuffle—well, it showed that celebrities knew a good hotel to scuffle in.)

"Housekeeper, please," the assistant manager said into the telephone on his desk. After a moment, he said, "This is Mr. Purdy, Mrs. MacReady. Will you have Mrs. Mason come down to my office, please. There's a man from the—"

He stopped with that, and listened. After a time he said, "Oh, hm-mm," and listened again. He said, "Yes, that was the right thing to do," and once more listened and then said, "No. I'll check on that." Then he replaced the receiver.

"This is most unfortunate," Mr. Purdy said. "It seems that Mrs. Mason didn't sign in at the proper time. And—I really can't understand this, Sergeant. But—"

The facts were not, however, difficult to understand. Sergeant Mullins understood them perfectly. Mrs. Mason had not reported for her tour of duty. A maid sent to her room found her not in it. She also found her possessions not in it. In simpler words, which Sergeant Mullins's mind readily supplied, Mrs. Gladys Mason had scrammed the hell out of there.

"Pine Room, please," the assistant manager said into his telephone. After a moment he said, "This is Mr. Purdy. Let me talk to Karl, will you?" While he waited he cupped a hand over the transmitter. "There's a son of hers," he said. "Working as a bus. Find out what he— Oh, Karl. You've got a bus named Mason. Son of one of the housekeepers. Wonder if you'd—" He stopped. He said, "Oh, hm-mm." He listened again. "All the same like mama, apparently," he said, and hung up and told Mullins what Mullins by then expected to hear.

Robert Mason had been due to report in the Pine Room at ten-thirty that morning to get to work, with other busboys, on setups for lunch. He had not.

"He live here too?" Mullins asked and Purdy looked surprised; said, "Certainly not, Sergeant. Probably has a furnished room somewhere. We can check his registered address." He was urged to do that, and did it by telephone. It took a little time. Robert Mason's listed address was in the West Forties—very much in the west of the Forties. Furnished rooms would come cheap there.

Purdy had been cooperative, unquestioning. He questioned now. "What's it all about, Sergeant?"

"Routine," Mullins told him. "Who'd know this Mrs. Mason best, would you say?"

Purdy shrugged at that, dissociating himself. He then considered. "I guess Ma MacReady," he said. "That's—Martha MacReady. We call her 'Ma.' She's the housekeeper. But I don't know how well—"

"Tell you what," Mullins said. "Suppose I talk to this Martha MacReady. Miss or missis?"

It was the latter. Her small office was down a long corridor and progress to it was impeded by hand trucks of laundry, ranged along one side of the corridor. Mrs. MacReady was pink and broad and comfortable behind a battered desk. She was using the telephone. She said, "Here's your check-out list. Got your pencil, dearie?" It appeared that dearie had her pencil. Mrs. MacReady gave a list of room numbers. Finished, she listened briefly. "Know it's long," she said. "Gladys has taken the day off, seems like. You just get the girls at it, dearie."

She hung up. She looked at Mullins. She said, "Well, you look like it." Mullins knew he looked like it. Sometimes it was a handicap, sometimes it wasn't. "My late was one of you," Mrs. MacReady said. "Patrolman. Happen you'd know him? Michael Mac-Ready. Coney Island Precinct last few years."

"Well, ma'am," Mullins said, "not offhand. Don't get out to Coney Island much."

"Before your time, anyway," Mrs. MacReady said, and since she appeared to be around sixty Mullins thought it likely. "What's Gladys Mason done?"

"Nothing we know of," Mullins said. "Just wanted a word with her. Looks like we're not going to get it right away, don't it? So, next best thing, what can you tell us about her? Except that she's not around?"

"She's a good sort," Mrs. MacReady said. "Whatever you say."

"Now ma'am," Mullins said, "I don't say she wasn't. How old would you say? How long's she worked here. Things like that."

The records in the employment office would show her age. "What she said it was, anyway." Mrs. MacReady herself would guess the middle forties. As for the length of time at the Dumont, a little over five years. "And," Mrs. MacReady said, "the best one I've got. Did have, I guess you'd say."

Mrs. Mason was a widow. "Most of them are, like me." Presumably, she had been a widow for some years. Before she came to the Dumont, she had worked, as a housekeeper, in other hotels. It was Mrs. MacReady's guess that she had started as a maid somewhere, and "been too good for it."

"She must have been pretty a while back," Mrs. MacReady said. "And, sort of high class, if you know what I mean. Come down in the world, like they say. Me, I was never up in it, you know. But sure you know."

"Sure," Mullins said. "This son of hers."

He was told he meant Bobby. He agreed he meant Bobby.

"Busboy, the poor kid," Mrs. MacReady said. "Wants to be a college graduate, but it looks as if that's out. Because here it is November and he's still working for Karl. And, let's face it, Karl's a holy terror if there ever was one."

"The headwaiter?"

Mullins had better not call Karl that to his face. Karl was maître d'.

"He sees a busboy, he steps on it," Mrs. MacReady said, unexpectedly.

She knew something of Robert Mason. At the request of his mother, she had helped him get his job at the Hotel Dumont, lowly as the job was. That had been the previous spring, when school closed. One of those colleges; she didn't know which one. Wouldn't mean anything to her, anyway. He was working his way through. "With what Gladys, the poor thing, could do to help." The job had, presumably, been only for the summer, for the school vacation. But here it was November. "And he's still lugging trays."

"Not now he isn't," Mullins said. "Anyway, today he isn't. Look. You think maybe Mrs. Mason got another job somewhere? And just lit out? With the kid? Look—maybe there's a hotel in the town the boy's school is in, and she got a job there. Could be?"

"For one thing," Mrs. MacReady said, "she's got money coming. For another thing, why'd she light out without telling anybody? This ain't a jail, Sergeant. I don't say it doesn't feel like it sometimes, but it ain't a jail. She wants to leave, she just says she wants to leave."

"What's the boy like?"

The boy was a good-looking kid, if you didn't mind them thin as rails. He was, at a guess, a little over twenty. "Only thing I noticed particularly," she said, "is that he sort of seemed to have his back up. Know what I mean? Sort of sore at everything. But a lot of kids are like that, nowadays."

"And don't we know it," Mullins said. "Bad-tempered, you'd call him?"

He could call it that. "More like surly," she said. "You know what I mean?"

Then she said, "What's it all about, Sergeant?"

"Routine," Mullins said, and was told to come off it. It was about this man Payne's getting killed, wasn't it? And what did that have to do with Gladys Mason.

"Well," Mullins said, "seems she might have heard something. That's all I know about it. They say, 'Go ask Mrs. Mason if she heard something.' You know how it is, your husband being on the cops. You suppose I could see her room?"

Mrs. MacReady didn't see why not, or what good it would do him. Mrs. Mason had taken everything when she went. But if he wanted . . .

The room on the seventeenth floor was very small—large enough for a cot-like bed, a chair, a small chest of drawers. Nothing in the drawers. A shallow closet off the room. Nothing in the closet. The bed unmade. No bath. The bath was down the hall. Not, clearly, a room for guests. A dormitory room, for help of the lower-middle echelon. On the street side.

Mullins leaned out of the single window. The room was at the side of the hotel and the entrance marquee was narrow. Looking down and to the side, Mullins could—just could—look under the marquee. He stood as far to one side as possible, and could see farther under the marquee. About, he judged, to the point at which Payne had been standing when he was shot. An uninterrupted line of vision equals, of course, an uninterrupted line of fire.

It is one thing to look around a room and find nothing useful in it. It is another thing to go over a room as experts go over a room. Mullins went back to Mrs. MacReady's office, and she said, "You again," which was what he had expected. She said, "Didn't find anything, did you?" and he admitted he hadn't.

"However," he said, "we'll want the technical-lab boys to go over it, and nobody to mess around in it first. O.K. And, how's to give me a description of Mrs. Mason? The boy, too, as well as you can."

"So," she said, "it's like that, is it. Well—"

Mrs. Mason, medium height. (If he knew what she meant. He did not, but nodded his head.) Weighed maybe a hundred and fifty. Light "complected." Yellowish sort of hair, but graying. Blue eyes. Sort of a round face, if he knew what she meant. "Didn't look very happy, most of the time." Pretty good figure, although she'd probably put on a few pounds. Dress her up, and give her something to smile about, and she'd be a good-looker still.

The boy—six feet, anyway, and thin as all get out. (Which was an expression Mullins hadn't heard for years.) Black hair, and it usually needed cutting. Face thin, like the rest of him. Eyes set way back in his head. As she had said, acted as if he had a chip on his shoulder, and looked like it, too. "I don't say," she added, "that a lot of girls wouldn't go for him. Give him sideburns and a *gui*tar."

Mullins stopped at Mr. Purdy's desk to repeat what he had said about Mrs. Mason's room. Purdy guessed it would be all right. Mullins regarded him briefly. "Sure, I'll see to it," Mr. Purdy said.

Mullins went crosstown to the far West Forties and up three flights of stairs which needed sweeping, breathing air that needed changing. The room the boy had had was small; it had a grimy window on an air shaft; it had a single light bulb depending from the ceiling. The room, like the only slightly larger room on the seventeenth floor of the Hotel Dumont, had been emptied.

The woman who, traced into basement lodgings, admitted she "ran the joint," was buxom, had very red lips and almost equally red cheeks and wore what

Mullins took to be a housecoat. She was very highly scented. She smiled brightly until Mullins identified himself. The smile disappeared, at that.

She didn't know anything about the kid; not a damned thing about the kid. He rented the room and that was the end of it. He had, that morning, told her he was leaving; he had carried a cheap suitcase; he had been wearing a raincoat, and dark trousers. He had been paid up to the end of the week and had tried to get a refund, and had been told no soap. He had not said why he was leaving, or where he was going.

"There'll be men around to go over the room," Mullins said. "Don't let anybody in it until they say it's O.K. Don't go in yourself."

"Listen, copper, I've got to make a living, don't I? Suppose somebody wants to rent—"

"You heard me," Mullins said. "Nobody. We'll make it as quick as we can."

Mullins took the Eighth Avenue subway to Twenty-third Street, and walked to 230 West Twentieth.

The girl had been in a great hurry to see James Self. That much was obvious. It was reasonably obvious, also, that she had wanted to get to Self to find out what Self had told a detective, had been asked by a detective. Which was entirely understandable; natural curiosity would take care of that. Only—had the girl been frightened? Or, Bill Weigand thought, am I riding a hunch to nowhere?

He walked through the Village street, seeking a telephone. It would be fine if, by now, precinct had come up with a sniper, complete with rifle, void of any motive for murder save a psychotic need to put bullets into people. Weigand could, then, quit bothering people who had cause to dislike Anthony Payne and free himself of the nagging suspicion that their causes were just. A burly, bearded novelist. A lean, unbearded bookseller. Two down (only by no means down) and how many more to go? A playwright-director who had expressed the wish that a collaborator drop dead. A handsome young actor who had lost his job but, conceivably, now gained more. (Nothing to prove that; merely something to be asked about.)

Bill found a drugstore, and a telephone booth. He got Stein. No sniper nabbed that Stein had heard of. Mullins was there, and Mrs. Mason, and also a son of hers, appeared to have taken a powder. Mrs. Gerald North had telephoned, and would call back. The bullet which had killed Payne had not been too badly damaged, so if they found a rifle they would know if it was the right rifle.

"I'll come in," Bill said, and went in.

The abrupt departure of Mrs. Mason and her son did not, Mullins pointed out, need to mean anything. That was, it presumably meant something—like, for example, Mrs. Mason having got a better job somewhere. Nothing, Mullins said he was saying, that would do them any good. But still—

"The descriptions are no good," Mullins said. "The kid—maybe, except there could be hundreds it would fit. And as for hers—thousands. Course, we can send a sketch man up and have him see what he can work out with Ma MacReady. Only, do we want her?"

Bill tapped his desk with active fingers. Mrs. Mason must have seen advantages in unannounced departure from the Dumont which outweighed the advantage of picking up money due her on the way. Another job seemed an insufficient advantage.

"She could have fired a gun from her room," Mullins said. "If she's good with a gun. The kid, I suppose, could have borrowed his mom's room. Only—why the hell?"

Bill couldn't help with that. He could, however, offer another suggestion.

Mrs. Lauren Payne was, perhaps, afraid she had, while under or partly under sedation, said something which would damage someone. Most likely, of course, would damage her herself. Pam North could remember nothing which might incriminate anybody. Possibly Mrs. Mason had heard more, or had a better memory.

"Yeah," Mullins said. "You think a payoff?"

A sufficient payoff, by Lauren Payne, for forgetfulness, for disappearance before memory was officially jogged, would, it was obvious, explain the abrupt departure of Mrs. Gladys Mason. It was reasonable that she might have taken her son along.

"The Paynes had a room overlooking the street," Bill said, and his drumming fingers paused briefly. "Fourth floor. She was in it—anyway, Payne told the Norths she had gone up to their room because she had a headache. Only—"

He looked across the room at a wall with a crack in it. He saw the front of the Hotel Dumont. He saw a narrow marquee, extending, to be sure, only a part of the distance from building to curb. But still—

"From Mrs. Mason's room," he said, "the marquee doesn't shield?"

"Nope," Mullins said. "Doesn't make it any easier. But somebody could shoot under it. If Payne was leaning the right way—"

"Give your friend Purdy a ring," Bill said. "Find out where the Paynes' room is. If it's in the middle of the building, above the marquee—"

Mullins got it. He reached for the telephone on

Weigand's desk, but at that moment it rang. "Get one outside," Mullins said, as Weigand reached to silence the shrill telephone. Bill nodded and said, "Weigand," and then, "Hello, Pam."

"Bill," Pam said, "she's one of the wives."

She paused, quite clearly in expectation of response—presumably of somewhat excited response.

Pamela North now and then comes up with answers to questions which have not yet been asked. She also draws conclusions from premises not stated. One can only explore.

"Who?" Bill said. "Of what wives?"

"And," Pam said, "she's the one who was with her after I was and—what did you say?"

"Only," Bill said, "who are we talking about, Pam? And, for that matter, what?"

She said, "Bill! Mr. Payne's murder, of course. About the housekeeper being one of his wives. The middle one, actually. After Faith and before Lauren. He says the son isn't his; but Faith thinks probably he is. Bill, Anthony Payne must have been really an awful man."

"Pam," Bill said, and spoke slowly. (The way to overtake Pamela North is sometimes to move very slowly indeed.) "Are you talking about Mrs. Mason? Mrs. Gladys Mason?"

"She spells it g-l-a-d-d-i-s," Pam said. "Of course."

"She doesn't now," Bill said. "If we're talking about the same woman. She was married to Payne? Her son is his son?"

"He denied it," Pam said. "When he was suing for the divorce. And, apparently, got a man to back him up. Hired the man, probably. And then didn't support either of them. So you see—"

"Pam," Bill said. "My dear—listen, Pam. Let's start at the beginning, shall we? The beginning was—"

"Oh," Pam said, "at Sardi's. But I don't see what real difference that—"

"Please," Bill said.

Pamela North can be patient with slow minds. She can be specific with those who must have each 't' crossed, 'i' dotted. She was a little disappointed in Bill Weigand, but she tempered the breeze.

"It does," she said when she had finished, "give you two more suspects, doesn't it? And I hope it isn't either of them, because if Faith is right they've had raw deals, haven't they?"

"Payne seems rather to have specialized in them," Bill said. "Mrs. Constable's reason for going to you, not to us—did it seem a little thin, Pam?"

"Not then," Pam said. "When I repeat it to you— perhaps. But—" She paused. "Of all of them," Pam said, "I'd think she had the least motive, Bill."

It was a jump again, but Bill could make this one with her. It might appear that Faith Constable was offering a red herring. But any obvious grudge Faith might have had against Payne must, surely, have grown threadbare with years. Any obvious grudge— One not obvious?

"Mrs. Mason and her son have disappeared, Pam," Bill said.

Pam said, "Oh," and sounded unhappy. Then she said, "Bill. The busboy I told you about? Who seemed to be—glaring at Tony Payne. Or, of course, at Jerry, but I didn't really think so. A tall, thin, dark boy. Was he—?"

"I think so," Bill said. "It fits together."

And Pamela North, again, said, "Oh," in the same tone and then, "I hope not, Bill." She paused. "I hope it will be a sniper. Don't you?"

It would, Bill agreed, be very convenient if it turned

out to be a sniper. He said they would have to keep on hoping. He said, "Listen, Pam. You won't—"

"Of course not," Pam North said. "Does Mrs. Payne—I mean the latest, of course—have a lot of money of her own?"

Bill Weigand flipped through his mind quickly. Somebody— Of course. Gardner Willings.

"I understand she has some," he said. "I don't know whether it's a lot. Why—?"

"Mink," Pam said. "Very minky mink. It probably doesn't matter. That is, obviously mink *does* matter. Can you and Dorian come by for a drink later?"

He chuckled at that. He said he didn't know; that he'd let her know if they could.

"For yourselves alone," Pam said "Don't laugh. Goodbye, Bill."

Sergeant Mullins came in after a few minutes. Bill had spent them looking at the crack in the wall opposite. He had let the information (which would have to be checked, of course) that Mrs. Payne had money of her own trickle through his mind. If she had enough— She would be free now to, among other things, marry somebody else—

The Paynes had had a two-room suite at the Hotel Dumont. It had been on the front. It had been on the fourth floor, well toward the right as one faced the building. Guessing, without seeing, Mullins supposed that someone who wanted to might have fired from the window of one of the rooms and sent a bullet under the marquee, into a selectd skull. If a good enough shot.

"The thing is, Loot," Mullins said, "she checked out just before noon." He sighed. "They don't seem to stay put, do they?"

The Paynes were registered as from Ridgefield, Connecticut. "Could be," Mullins said, "she just went home. I asked the State cops to make a check, just for the fun of it. O.K.?"

"Right," Bill said.

"Live on something called Nod Road," Mullins said. "Funny thing to call a road, isn't it? Was that Mrs. North phoned?"

His tone was not exactly accusing. Sergeant Mullins does not really share Inspector O'Malley's view of Mr. and Mrs. North. On the other hand, where the Norths are screwiness is.

Bill said yes, and told Mullins what Mrs. North had called about.

Mullins considered.

"You know," he said, "that's not so screwy, is it? When you think the kid wants to go to college and apparently they can't swing it? And he sees his old man—what mama tells him is his old man, anyway—rolling in it? And his mother's had a dirty deal and—" He paused. "It's not really screwy at all, is it, Loot?"

9

Facts are collected; they are poured into a mind and shaken together, in the hope of a precipitate. But some facts are hunches only; some facts are, at best, splinters from the truth. Where a man was at a certain time may be a fact. But who the man was, what kind of man he was, may be of far greater importance, and that can never be more than guessed at, with guesses formulated under conditions necessarily adverse. Almost no one is quite himself while being interrogated by a policeman. Some who are normally mild turn belligerent; the pugnacious may grow wary. Criminal investigation has been loosely compared to many things, including the putting together of a jigsaw puzzle. It is seldom that simple. The pieces of such a puzzle are of fixed shape, immutable. Men and women change shape when touched.

William Weigand gazed at a wall with a crack in the plaster and thought about men and women, and waited for the Connecticut State Police to pass along information which would, in all probability, prove irrelevant. If Mrs. Lauren Payne preferred her home to a hotel room while she wrapped grief around her—always assuming she had grief to wrap—there was no reason to suppose it would mean anything. Or, for that matter, would it mean anything if she were not in a house on a road called Nod. She might have gone anywhere—to friends or relatives; to another hotel less memory-haunted. Nobody had told her to stay put.

The trooper who had driven from the Ridgefield Barracks to Nod Road to see whether Mrs. Payne had come home was only one of a good many men busy that November afternoon turning over stones to see what might be under them. Two men went through files of the Supreme Court, State of New York, seeking records in the case of Payne vs. Payne, handicapped by the fact that the year of the hearing was not precisely known and of the two who could have precisely given it, one was dead and the other missing. A man with a sketch pad in hand sat with a large pink woman in a small office at the end of a long, dim corridor and made pencil lines on paper and said, "Is this more like it, Mrs. MacReady? Or are the eyebrows more like this?" When he had finished with that, he would go to another part of the hotel and say much the same things to someone else, most probably a busboy. "Begin to look like him now, would you say? Different about the mouth, huh? More like this, maybe?"

Men blew dust on objects in a room on the seventeenth floor of the Hotel Dumont and blew it off again, and did the same in a tiny, almost airless room in a tenement in the West Forties. And men also used vacuum cleaners in both rooms, sucking dust up once more.

Men from the Third Detective District, Eighteenth Precinct, had the longest, the most tedious, job. At the

Hotel Dumont there had, at the time in issue, been twenty-three overnighters, counting couples as singular. These included, as one, Mr. and Mrs. Anthony Payne, who had checked in a little after noon the day before, and had not checked out together. But Gardner Willings was not included; he had been at the Dumont for almost a week. There was, of course, no special reason to believe that the man or woman they sought had stayed only overnight at the hotel. The twenty-three (or twenty-two with the Paynes themselves omitted) provided merely a place to start, and their identification was the barest of starts. With names and addresses listed, verification came next. It would take time; it would, almost inevitably, trouble some water. ("I certainly was not at the Dumont last night and my husband couldn't have been. He's in Boston. Of *course* he's in—")

The Hotel King Arthur across the street provided almost twice as many problems. The King Arthur offered respectable and convenient lodgings to people from the suburbs who wanted to see a show and didn't want—heaven knew didn't want!—to lunge anxiously through crowded streets to railroad stations and, at odd hours of night, drive from smaller stations to distant homes, probably through rain or, in November, something worse. The King Arthur was less expensive than the Dumont. The King Arthur had fifty-four overnighters, again counting rooms rather than people.

Check the overnighters out. Failing to find what was wanted, as was most likely, check out other guests, with special—but not exclusive—attention to those with rooms on the street. (Anyone active enough can reach a roof, wherever his room may be.) And know, while all this went on, that there was no real reason to suppose that the murderer had been a guest in either hotel. It was not even certain the shot had been fired from either hotel. There were other roofs, less convenient but not impossible. It is dull business, detecting, and hard on feet.

There was also the one salient question to ask, and ask widely: Did you notice anything out of the way? Like, for example, a man carrying a twenty-two rifle, probably with a telescopic sight attached?

There was, of course, no hope it really would be that simple. The sniper, whether psychopathic marksman or murderer by intent, would hardly have walked to his vantage point with rifle over shoulder, whistling a marching tune. Anybody carrying anything that might hide a rifle? Long thin suitcase? Or long fat suitcase, for that matter? Shrugs met that, from room clerks, from bellhops. Who measures? But nothing, it appeared, long enough to attract attention. Cases, say, for musical instruments? None noted at the Dumont. Several at the King Arthur. A combo was staying there. And had been for a week. Anything else? Anything at all? Shrugs met that.

(Detective Pearson, Eighteenth Precinct, thought for a time he might be on to something. A refuse bin at the Dumont turned up a florist's box—a very long box for very long-stemmed flowers. Traces of oil on green tissue? The lab to check. The lab: Sorry. No oil.)

Anything at all strange?

Well, a man had tried, at the King Arthur, to register with an ocelot. At the Dumont, a guest had come in a collapsible wheel chair. At the King Arthur one guest had had his head heavily bandaged, and another had a bandaged foot and had walked with crutches. There had also been a man who must have had St. Vitus or something, because he kept jerking his head.

As reports dribbled in, William Weigand tossed them into the certrifuge which had become his head.

Mullins came in. There was no sign of Mrs. Lauren Payne at her house on Nod Road, Ridgefield, Connecticut. The house was modern, large, on five acres. Must have cost plenty. The State cops would check from time to time; pass word when there was word to pass. Weigand tossed this news into the centrifuge. Sort things out, damn it. Sort out the next move.

Try to forget motive for the moment. Consider opportunity. Only those actually with Payne when he was shot, or who had left the party within not more than five minutes (make five arbitrary) positively had none. The Norths; Hathaway, Jerry's publicity director; Livingston Birdwood, producer of *Uprising*. They had been with Payne when he was shot, could not therefore have shot him from above.

Take Gardner Willings. He had left after the scuffle; had been seen to leave. He would have had ample time to go into a blind somewhere and wait his prey. Consider him seriously, therefore? Intangibles entered, then—hunches which felt like facts. Willings would ambush, certainly; Willings undoubtedly had. Willings was, presumably, a better than average shot. But—hunch, now—Willings would not ambush anything which went on two legs instead of four. Because, if for no other reason, Willings would never for a moment suppose he was not bigger, tougher, than anything else that went on two legs. Ambushes are laid by those who doubt themselves, as any man may against a tiger.

Faith Constable had had to "go on" from the party and had, presumably, gone on. To be checked out further. Forget motive? No, motive is a part of fact. Nobody in his right mind punishes a quarter-century-old dereliction. Grudges simply do not keep that well in a sane mind. Faith Constable had accomplished much in a quarter of a century. Jeopardize it now to correct so old a wrong? Bill shook his head. Also, he thought, I doubt if she could hit the side of a barn with a shotgun.

Lauren herself? She had left the party early, pleading a headache. No lack of opportunity, presuming she had a gun. She might, conceivably, have brought one in in a large-enough suitcase. (Check on the Payne luggage.) She might now have taken it away again. Motive—her husband wandering? Bitter, unreasoning jealousy? Heaven knew it happened and hell knew it too. But—it happened, almost always, among the primitive and, usually, among the very young. (Call it mentally young; call it retarded.) There was nothing to indicate that Lauren Payne was primitive. She did not move in primitive circles. She was young, but not that young.

It occurred to Bill Weigand that he was, on a hunch basis, eliminating a good many. He reminded himself that he had an unusual number of possibilities.

The Masons, mother or son, or mother *and* son? Opportunity was obvious. Motive. Here, too, the cause to hate lay well back in the years. But bitterness had more cause to remain, even increasingly to corrode. With the boy, particularly. The boy had, apparently—if Mrs. MacReady was right in what she had told Mullins—only in recent months been forced to give up college, to work as a busboy. Seeing the man he blamed for this made much of—youth and bitterness and—

Bill picked up the telephone; got Mullins.

"Send out a pickup on Mrs. Mason and the boy when you've got enough to go on," Bill said. "Right?"

Mullins would do.

A man named Lars Simon, playwright-director, had expressed a wish that Anthony Payne drop dead. He would say, of course, that he had not really had any such wish; that what he had said was no more than one of those things one does say, lightly, meaning nothing. Which probably would turn out to be true; which he obviously had to be given the opportunity to say.

A man named Blaine Smythe, with "y" and "e" but pronounced without them, had been fired at Payne's insistence. He was also, if Pam North was right, a closer acquaintance of Lauren Payne's than she, now, was inclined to admit. He might deny the latter; would certainly deny any connection between the two things, or any connection of either with murder. He would have to be given the opportunity.

Mullins? It was evident that Mullins was the man to go. It was evident that a captain should remain at his desk, directing with a firm hand and keeping a firm seat. Bill Weigand was good and tired of the wall opposite, and the crack in the plaster. Let Mullins keep the firm seat; let Stein.

When Siamese cats are intertwined it is difficult to tell where one leaves off and another begins. Stilts and Shadow, on Pam's bed, appeared to be one cat—rather large, as Siamese cats go, and, to be sure, having two heads and two tails. On the other hand, they, or it, seemed to have no legs whatever. Pamela North said, "Hi," to her cats, and added that proper cats met their humans at the door. Of four dark brown ears, one twitched slightly at this. "All right," Pam said. "I know it isn't dinnertime."

But at this the one too-large cat suddenly became two cats, stretching. Shadow, the more talkative, began at once to talk, her voice piteous. Stilts, a more direct cat, leaped from the bed and trotted briskly toward the kitchen. Shadow looked surprised, wailed, and trotted after her. The hell it isn't dinnertime, two waving tails told Pam North.

117

It was not, whatever tale was told by tails. Martha presumably would cope. She might be firm. It was most unlikely that she would be firm. They want to be fat cats, Pam thought, and lighted a cigarette and leaned back on a chaise and considered pulling her thoughts together. After a time, it occurred to her that her thoughts were not worth the trouble. A vague feeling that Anthony Payne had had it coming was hardly a thought and was, in any event, reprehensible. Had Faith Constable's explanation of her confidence, so uninvited, been a little thin? That was more like a thought, but not a great deal more. Had that tall dark boy, carrying trays too heavy for him, found what he might have considered adulation of a man he probably hated more than he could bear? And possessed himself—how?—of a rifle and killed? Pam found she had no answers; had only a hope. The poor kid—the poor, frail kid. Some people have luck and some have no luck and that, whatever people who prefer order say, is the size of it. The poor, unlucky—

The telephone rang. Pam realized, to her surprise, that she had been almost dozing. At four o'clock in the afternoon. Two martinis for lunch—that was the trouble. I ought to remember. Don't pretend. You do remember. You just—"Hello? Yes, this is she? What?"

The voice had music in it. Even with words coming too fast, they came on the music of the voice.

"I said I would," Pam said. "They won't talk about who gave the information. Not unless they have to. They don't, Mrs. Constable. Not unless they have—"

She was interrupted.

"Call this a cry for help," Faith Constable said. "It's unjustified—perhaps it's inexcusable. But—somebody has to help. And I—I just don't know how. She's come to me and I—in this sort of thing I'm nothing. Nothing at all. And—she's so frightened. So frightened and so helpless. You—maybe you'll know how to help. I know we've no right. No right at all. But—"

"Who?" Pam said.

"Gladys Mason. The boy—she can't find Bobby— Will you come and help?"

This is entirely preposterous, Pamela North thought, in a taxi, traveling uptown. Just because once we found a body in a bathtub. I should just have said, "Oh, excuse me," and closed the door. If I had, people wouldn't now keep on thinking, whatever we tell them, that Jerry and I are some sort of detectives and I wouldn't, now, with my sympathies all stirred up—the poor kid; the poor lost kid!—be in this taxi; be sticking my neck out again. I'd be home, having a long shower, and telling Martha that Captain and Mrs. Weigand may drop in for a drink and—

On the other hand, Pam thought, we wouldn't know Bill and Dorian, and I can't think of any two people we'd rather know. There is really no sense in trying to make sense out of things. "The moving finger," Pam thought and, unknowingly, said. To which the cab driver said, "What you say, lady? Moving as fast as I can. This time of day—"

"I know," Pam said.

"Seems like it gets worse every day," the cab driver said. "I'll tell you what it is. It's all these private cars. You'd think they'd have enough sense to—"

Pam agreed. She agreed that somebody ought to do something. She agreed that, in addition to being too numerous, most private drivers oughtn't to be allowed to have licenses. She agreed.

"Here we are, lady," the cab driver said, and stopped, as near to the curb as he could get, in front of a tall and narrow house in the East Sixties.

A maid in a gray uniform answered the door while Pam's finger still was on the bell-push. She said, "Mrs. North?" before Pam could say anything. She said, "Mrs. Constable is expecting you, Mrs. North. If you'll come up?"

The maid led the way up narrow stairs which hugged a wall. On the second floor she led only a few steps to an open door, and said, "Mrs. North, Mrs. Constable," and stepped back to let Pam go into a long, high room. At the end of the room dark curtains were drawn to cover two high windows; a fire was bright in a fireplace under a black marble mantel; tall table lamps lighted the room softly. The room's carpet was soft under Pam's feet.

Mrs. Constable sat behind a table, and behind a tea service—a silver service which glowed in the soft light. She stood up when Pam came into the room and said, "My dear. So good of you."

It was all most unexpected, although Pam would have found it difficult to say what she had expected. Only, somehow—not this. Not this quiet serenity; this soothing dignity. A guest welcomed to tea in surroundings which could only, if reluctantly, be called elegant; an expected guest with unhurried, assured, graciousness. How uncouth of me, Pam thought briefly, to picture myself as sticking my neck out. How, in a word, vulgar.

"Good afternoon, Mrs. Constable," Pam said, and looked again around the room. "Such a lovely room," she said. Then, in response to smile, the most delicate of directing gestures, Pam sat in a chair beside the fireplace, facing Faith Constable. "This is Mrs. Mason," Faith Constable said. "This is Mrs. North, Gladys."

The woman who sat, deeper in the room, in a chair

which faced the fireplace repeated Pam's name. And her voice shook.

"There, dear," Mrs. Constable said, gently, and poured tea. The maid had come into the room, moving very quietly. She took tea to the woman who faced the fireplace; to Pamela. She offered thin sandwiches. In the dim light to which her eyes were growing accustomed, Pam could see that, as she took the cup, Gladys Mason's hand shook a little. A little of the tea spilled into the saucer. Pam looked up at the maid and smiled and said, "Thank you."

Gladys Mason wore a black dress; a very plain black dress which had, somehow, the appearance of a uniform. Pam, again, sought words in her own mind. A "serviceable" black dress. She wore a small black hat on light hair—hair a grayish blond. Her face was round. From its shape, it should have been a comfortable face. It was drawn. Lines dipped from the corners of the small, pretty mouth. When she was younger she must have had a lovely figure, Pam North thought. Must have had a pretty face.

"It begins to get dark so early now, doesn't it?" Mrs. Constable said and then, "Thank you, Norton." The maid said, "Yes, Mrs. Constable," and went out of the dignified room. There was a little pause, a little sipping of tea.

"It's hard to know where to begin," Mrs. Constable said. "We need—advice. Gladys came to me because—"

"I shouldn't have," Gladys Mason said. Her voice, Pam thought, was raised a little above its ordinary pitch. "I realize I shouldn't have. Only—" She stopped. She swallowed as if muscles ached from swallowing. "There isn't anybody," she said, and now her voice was lower; now her voice was dull.

"There never has been. Never—never anybody."

"Dear," Faith Constable said. "Don't say things like that. They're not—"

"Oh," Gladys Mason said. "It's true. I've no right to come to you. Least of all to you. You did so much when—when you had no reason to do anything. When you had reason—"

"Nonsense," Faith said and for the first time the subdued atmosphere was altered. Faith did not speak sharply, yet the effect was of a word spoke sharply. "Come to that, we were birds of a feather. Plucked. Mrs. North—" She paused. "Last names are awkward," she said. "For me. In the profession we're so—" She raised expressive shoulders.

"Pamela," Pam North said. "Although, usually, just Pam."

"Gladys's son has disappeared," Faith said. "She's worried. She can't—and she really can't—go to the police. It's not as it was with me. Not just—not wanting to."

"But nobody else—" Pam said and stopped because Faith put down her teacup and shook her head slowly, with finality. Faith looked at Gladys Mason and, clearly, waited. For all her slight grace, her shimmer (apparent even now), Faith Constable was the strong one, Pam thought. Now, without a word, she commanded.

"There's nothing anybody can do," Gladys said, in a dull voice. "I realize that. It's—" And then, quite unexpectedly, she put her own teacup down and moved as if about to stand up. And again, and this time there was real sharpness in the word, Faith said, "Nonsense." And this time she commanded with the word, and Gladys Mason leaned back in the chair and looked at the bright leaping of the fire. No, Pam thought, looked toward it. Pam was conscious of a

122

kind of embarrassment, of unease. I'm being pulled into something, Pam thought. Mrs. Mason doesn't want me to be pulled into it. And yet, in a way, does.

"She thinks," Faith said, "that the police are looking for her son. His name's Robert. Bobby. Or—she thinks he's running and that they will be looking when they find that out. Because—" She looked again at Gladys Mason. There was a considerable pause. Mrs. Mason continued to look toward the dance of little flames which, Pam was sure, she did not really see.

"I'm afraid," the woman in a black dress said, very slowly, toward the fireplace. "Afraid they will find out—I mean will think—he killed—" Again there were seconds of silence. "Killed his father," she said. She stopped once more. Faith looked at Pam and her look said, "You heard. Don't let her stop now." Pam almost could hear the words.

"Find out?" Pam said. "What do you mean, Mrs. Mason? You speak as if—"

"I'm afraid," Gladys Mason said. "Just—I don't know. I don't really believe it and he says—" She made her first gesture. It was to spread her hands. Small and well-shaped hands. And reddened hands. She looked at Faith. "All right," she said. "I've gone this far. Come to you. And now, to a—a stranger. All right. I'll tell her." Then, and this also was for the first time, she turned in her chair so that she looked directly at Pam North. "I think Lauren saw him from her room," she said. "Lauren Payne. Going in across the street. She said—it was after you had gone—"

Once started, she told it, for the most part, simply enough.

10

After Mrs. North, the night before, had told Lauren Payne what had happened, Mrs. Mason had been called in. "Nobody knew, you see," she said. "I was just—a kind of servant. That there was any connection—"

At first, Lauren Payne had seemed to respond quickly and quite simply to the sedative the house physician had given her. After some ten minutes, Mrs. Mason had begun to think she might safely leave. And then Lauren had started to talk. It was as if she were talking in her sleep. The words were hurried, indistinct and, at first, they did not seem relevant to one another. "I couldn't make any sense out of them." But then, after a few minutes, Lauren had spoken more clearly. In a sentence—in part of a sentence.

"The first time, I wasn't really listening. But then she said it over and over and—"

"He's not supposed to be over there," Lauren had

124

said; had said several times. "And there's something
the matter with his leg. But there's—it's part of—"

The unfinished sentence, of course, did not make
sense. But Mrs. Mason, now, was quite sure that
that—well, almost certainly that—was what Lauren
had said. Then she had repeated, several times, that he
was not supposed to be "over there."

"At first," Gladys Mason said, "I thought she might
be trying to tell me something. I don't think she was,
really. Probably she didn't even know, then, that there
was anybody else there. But before I was sure of that,
I said, 'Over where, Mrs. Payne?' When I said it the
first time she didn't seem to hear me. But I asked her
again and then she said, quite clearly, not at all as if
she was talking in her sleep, 'The King Arthur, of
course.' But then she went back to—it was like mum-
bling. She said, 'He doesn't belong there. He's not
supposed—why's he going over there?' "

Gladys Mason said that then she was "worried."
She did not immediately say what in these words had
worried her. Gladys had said, "Who do you mean,
dear?" and had got no answer. She had said, guessing,
"You were looking out the window, Mrs. Payne?" and
was answered.

"She seemed to keep going in and out," Gladys
Mason said. "One time it would be just sleep talking.
But then it was as if she were perfectly awake. When I
asked if she had been looking out her window—the
window of her room, across the street toward the
other hotel—she said, 'Of course,' as if I should have
known." Gladys Mason paused. "Her room is on the
front of the hotel," she said. "Of the Dumont. She
could have looked directly across the street. Seen
anything."

"But I don't," Pam said, and Faith, just perceptibly,
shook her head. "Did she see whoever it was fire the

shot?" Pam said. "Was that what—" Faith shook her head again, but this time Pam ignored the movement. "Worried you?" Pam said. "Did she say she saw your son?"

"No," Gladys said. "Not that. She didn't say that. Only, don't you see, she saw him—I mean, someone— going into the King Arthur. Somebody who wasn't 'supposed' to go there. She might have meant, didn't belong there."

"Did she know your son, Mrs. Mason? As your son, I mean?"

Mrs. Mason's hands moved, again, in a helpless gesture. She didn't know.

"But Anthony might have—pointed him out," she said. "Anthony knew he was working in the hotel. I—" She broke off. She looked at nothing. When she spoke, it was as if she spoke to nobody. "I did— something I'm ashamed of," she said, to nobody. "A humiliating thing. When—when we ran out of money, so Bobby couldn't go back to school, I wrote his father. Asked him to help. Only to help a little. I thought—thought he might have changed. It was a begging letter. But Bobby's his son. His *son*. He even looks like his father a little—the way his father was then."

She paused again.

"He hadn't changed," she said. "He didn't even answer. But he would only have had to see Bobby to know who he was and—he may have pointed him out to her. It would have been like Anthony. Pointed him out to her and laughed about it and said—I don't know what he would have said. Something that was cruel. And—something that wasn't true." She turned, abruptly, to Faith Constable. She said, "You told Mrs. North, didn't you?" Faith nodded her head.

"He was a cruel man," Gladys Mason said. "Even

when—when there was no need to be cruel. People say now that things aren't really black and white, and I suppose they aren't. Only, sometimes they are. He was cruel because—because he enjoyed it. He wanted to get rid of me." She hesitated, looking toward the fire. "He'd had what he wanted of me. All right. That happens to people. I was a silly little thing—a pretty, silly little thing." She shook her head, and smiled faintly, the light on her face flickering as the little flames danced in the grate. "It's like it was somebody else," she said. "A girl who didn't like her name— didn't like the looks of her name—thought it was an ordinary name. And so— I used to spell it g-l-a-d-d-i-s. You can see what—what the girl was. And I was flattered and—oh, he said all sorts of things." She looked at Faith Constable.

"I can well imagine," Faith said.

"He could have gone somewhere where it's easy," Gladys said. "Or, had me go. I'd have gone. It was—I suppose it was more fun for him the way he did it. Hiring this man—a man I'd only met a few times, and never alone—to lie about me. To say—to say Bobby was his son, not my husband's. Or—oh, there wasn't any end to it. *Could* have been his son. As if there might have been—" She broke off.

Pam thought, at first, that she was not going to go on with it; wished she would not go on with it; wanted to say, "Please don't. You're only hurting yourself. I believe you. Please don't." To say, "It was all long ago. Please don't."

"Bobby is his son. He couldn't have been anyone else's. There were other people who lied, who said Anthony was on the West Coast at—at the right time. He was, but not all the time. He—he came back. He— came back. Bobby's his son. God knows, if he weren't I'd be—be glad. Yes, I'd be *glad*. Particularly now."

Suddenly, she put her hands in front of her face; covered her eyes with reddened fingers.

If her boy had killed, it was his father he had killed. The hands were raised to shut that knowledge out.

I wish this would stop, Pam thought. This *has* to stop.

"When he was old enough, he began to hate Anthony," Gladys said. "Oh, I told him too much. I was still young and bitter and I told him too much. And—and everything was bad for us for a long time. I was no good at anything and—with a baby. Faith, if you hadn't—why did you?"

"Bird of a feather," Faith said. "It doesn't matter now. It was nothing. And, dear, do you have—?"

Gladys Mason had asked a question but she had not listened to the answer. Pam North was sure of that; sure that she, far away in bitter memories, had merely waited for the older woman to finish speaking.

"He hated his father," Gladys said. "We both did. And—and he wouldn't accept anybody else. After a time it seemed to me that he wouldn't accept *any*body. Not even, part of the time, me. Mr. Mason tried. Even got Bobby to take his name. Mr. Mason was—he was all right. Meant to be kind. He tried for a while but—it was hard to be patient. For him. Then he died and—"

She is, Pam thought, trying to make us see a boy growing up in hatred. She hasn't the words, Pam thought. All the words she has are the ordinary words. She's trying to explain, extenuate. She is quite sure he killed his father. But, merely because—?

"So many things were wrong," Gladys said, and now it seemed that she was, in essence, talking to herself; explaining, to herself, what had gone wrong with her life, and with a boy's life. "He grew too fast. When he was twelve he was taller than I am. And so thin. Always so thin. And—bitter. And, there was always something else." She broke off, and looked at Faith, then at Pam, as if she had, until that moment, forgotten they were there.

"You want me to stop," she said. "Not to—to drag you through this. To burden you with it."

God knows, Pam thought. But she shook her head.

"Only," Gladys Mason said, "it's part of—of everything. I'm afraid it is. The other thing, he was sort of ashamed. I suppose you'd call it that. Felt he wasn't as good as other people. Because—oh, of everything that had happened. A boy starts wrong—a boy who's thin-skinned—" She paused again.

"Anyway," she said, "he got this awful need to be as good as anybody—better than anybody. He tried to do things he wasn't meant to do. Play football, even. In high school he tried to play football. That was how he hurt his knee, you know."

Pam looked quickly at Faith Constable. Faith, just perceptibly, touched her lips.

"It's only when he's tired that he limps at all," Gladys said. "Tired or—or worked up about something. One doctor said there isn't really anything the matter with his knee. Not really. That it's because—oh, a lot of rigamarole. He found he couldn't play football as well as the other boys and had to find a reason and— People make things up. He hurt his knee. That's all it was. Not anything—queer."

The shape formed slowly; it was a little as if smoke took shape, formed a pattern. Or as if a cloud took shape against the sky. "Something the matter with his leg." A tall young man she knew, perhaps only by sight, limping. A thing for Lauren Payne to notice, since he did not always limp.

It had been worse recently for the boy, Gladys Mason told them, talking some of the time to the two women who sat on either side of a flickering fire, some

129

of the time seemingly only to herself. They had thought they could find the money to send him to college, partly from what she could provide, partly from what he could earn himself. He had gone a year; was to have returned in September.

A job he had hoped to get in the college town he hadn't got. She herself had had to go to a doctor. "It turned out to be nothing, but I had to pay just the same." Going to college had had to be given up. "Only for this year I kept telling him. And he said, 'Don't fool yourself, Mom. You're not fooling me.' " She looked at the fire for a moment. "Being a busboy was the worst thing that could have happened," she said. "A busboy—well, there's almost nothing below a busboy. If you want to be a hotel man I suppose it's different. Just by itself—" She made a dismissing gesture with her hands. And, for a moment, it seemed that she had finished telling them what she had to tell.

The shape was still vague, Pam thought. A bitter boy with a limp. A boy who might—but there was no real proof of that—have been seen going into a hotel where he did not belong; a hotel from which (but even that, so far as Pam knew, was not certain) a shot might have been fired. There must, obviously, be more, since, obviously, Gladys Mason believed, and was fighting against believing, her son to be a murderer.

"He said he sold it," Gladys Mason said, and spoke suddenly. "If he really sold it, and can prove he did. But then, why would he run away?"

Pam looked at Faith Constable and Faith shook her head and, slightly, raised her shoulders.

"Sold what, Mrs. Mason?" Pam said.

For a moment, it seemed that the question surprised the black-clad woman. But then she said, "Oh, didn't I tell you about that? About the rifle?"

"No."

"At college," Mrs. Mason said. "He couldn't play the rough games. Because of his knee, you know. But—I suppose you'd say—he had to prove himself. There was a rifle team. Rifle club, or something. He bought a rifle—not a good one, he said. A cheap rifle, secondhand. But—he got to be very good with it. Better than the others. He was—it was good for him, for a while. Being better at something. But then—I don't know—it seemed just to wear off. Anyway, he says he sold the rifle. Months ago. He'd be able to prove that, wouldn't he?"

"I'd think so," Pam said. "When did he tell you this? About selling the rifle?"

"Why, last night."

They could only wait. She said she had thought she had told them. "Only me," Faith said. "Tell Pamela."

Mrs. Mason had been on duty until eight o'clock the night before. After she had finished, had gone to her room, she had increasingly worried about what Lauren Payne had said, become increasingly convinced that it meant what she feared it meant. She had left her room and gone across town to the room her son lived in and found him there. He was "excited, worked up" but, when she told him what she was afraid of, and what Lauren Payne had said, he had denied "that he'd done anything wrong." He had said that nobody could prove he had "just because I wanted to." He had said he had sold the rifle a long time ago. He had told her she mustn't worry.

"I wanted to believe him. I—I *do* believe him. Only—he seemed so strange, so excited."

Not in words, only in mind. She had not believed him. She had kept on trying, but she had not believed him.

131

He telephoned her the next morning—that morning. He said he was going away, and that she shouldn't worry. Going away until it "blew over."

"He still sounded—strange. I don't know—terribly excited. I told him he mustn't do that; told him to wait. When he wouldn't, I told him I'd come and join him— bring him money. That wherever we went we'd go together. He said it would be better if I didn't but— finally I thought I'd persuaded him. I said I'd meet him at Grand Central and he said, all right, at about noon, then, at the information desk. So I put my things in a suitcase—I haven't got many things—and went down the stairs, because I thought they might already be looking for him—that she might have told somebody else—and if they saw me they would follow me. But—"

But Robert Mason had not showed up at the information booth at Grand Central—not at noon, and not by one o'clock, and not by two. Gladys Mason had put her suitcase in a locker then and had gone a few places she thought her son might be. "He had some friends he'd told me about. Not many. Most of them weren't in their rooms and nobody who was had seen him. So—I didn't have anybody, know anybody to go to. I couldn't go to the police and ask them to find him. I couldn't—"

She leaned back in her chair as if very tired.

"I came here," she said. "I hadn't any right, but I came here."

She had, it appeared, simply done that—come to the narrow house in the East Sixties as to sanctuary. Faith Constable had not been there; she had been at rehearsal. The maid Norton had telephoned the theater.

Now, with her story told, Gladys Mason seemed merely to wait. She waited, Pam thought, to be told what to do. Pam had, also, an unhappy feeling that

Faith Constable was waiting too—waiting for Pamela North to point out a course of action. Really, Pam North thought. Of all things!

"More tea?" Faith Constable said. "It may not be very hot. I can have Norton—"

"I'm sure it will be all right," Pam said, glad she was sure of something. Faith started to get up, but Pam carried her cup to the tea table. Gladys Mason seemed not to have heard the offer of more tea.

What I should tell her to do is obvious, Pam thought, sipping tea which was just barely warm enough. I should tell her to go to the police, explain everything to them. If the boy didn't—

She broke that thought off. For one thing, Mrs. Mason would not go to the police, and could not be expected to go to the police, however fully the logic of such an action might be explained. And, there was hesitation in Pam's own mind. She was, at first, surprised to find it there. Then she was not surprised. If Bill could be the one to find the boy, or Stein could. Or, for that matter, Mullins. And there were, of course, many others.

But few policemen are psychologists and almost none psychiatrists. Something of that sort might be needed here—at the least what might be needed here would be gentleness, a desire to understand. These qualities of mind are by no means universal, and a policeman's trade is unlikely to encourage them. In recent years, particularly, policemen have had little time to spend in consideration of the vagaries of the young mind. The vagaries of young action have kept a good many policemen very busy.

If we could find the boy first, Pam thought. Talk to him. The poor, unhappy kid—the lost kid. Running now. But—running from the police? Or, from everything—from defeat and loneliness; perhaps even from his own mother's inability to believe? Find him and—

My neck again, Pam thought. Stuck out again. Oh, damn it all. "Lame dogs over stiles," Jerry would say—had so often had occasion to say. "Show Pam a lame dog," he had told Bill Weigand once, "and she'll find a stile to help it over. Hell, she'll build one. And sly dogs begin to limp when they see her." All right, Pam thought, I'm the way I am.

It was she, now, who was looking toward the fire, not at it. The other two waited, now, for her, Faith looking at her, Gladys, still leaning back in her chair, seeming to look at nothing. Merely waiting to be told.

Only, Pam thought, we can't find him. How can we find him? So, what can we really—

"Of course," Pam said, "we don't really know whether there's anything in this, do we? Because we don't know what Mrs. Payne meant to say. We're only—guessing. Perhaps she was talking about somebody entirely different. Perhaps about some*thing* entirely different. Not about the murder at all."

They listened. Gladys even leaned forward in her chair to listen.

"She came to me this morning," Pam said. "She thought she might have said something; that she didn't remember what she had said. When she was groggy from the stuff. She hadn't, to me. And she didn't know, or wouldn't tell me, what kind of thing she was afraid she'd said. I thought afraid. As if she thought she might have incriminated somebody. Wait! *Somebody important to her.* And your son, Mrs. Mason, wouldn't have been that. At least—would he?"

"No," Gladys Mason said. "Only—only to me."

"So," Pam said, "all we have to do is to call her up and ask. Because not remembering what she said is one thing, and what she saw is another, isn't it?"

Faith Constable's expressive eyes flickered for a

moment. But then she nodded. "Over there," she said, and pointed toward shadows.

There was no question—except momentarily in Pam's own mind—that Pamela North would be the person to telephone and ask Lauren Payne what, if anything, she had seen the evening before. She found the telephone in the shadows; dialed the number Gladys Mason gave her, heard "Hotel Dumont, good afternoon," and asked for Mrs. Anthony Payne. She heard "One moment, please," but it was more than a moment. Then Pam listened again, and said, "Oh," and hung up.

Mrs. Anthony Payne had checked out of the Hotel Dumont. It was rather like reaching a foot up for a final stair-tread which isn't there. Pam went back to her chair and sipped tea which was no longer warm at all. I don't, she thought, really like tea. The idea of tea is wonderful but tea, when all's said and done, is only tea.

"They have a house in a place called Ridgefield," Gladys Mason said. "There was a picture of it in a magazine. Anthony in sports clothes." She paused. "Trying," she said, "to look like a man who likes roses. Ridgefield, Connecticut."

It took longer to find a telephone number, through information—through information which at first reported no Anthony Payne listed in Ridgefield, New Jersey, and said, "Oh," with some indignation and, after what seemed a longish time for research, reported an Idlewood number with detachment, and in a tone of considerable doubt. (The doubt, Pam realized, was of the mental capacity of someone who did not know the difference between New Jersey and Connecticut.)

Pam dialed and waited and listened to the signal which meant the distant ringing of a telephone bell.

She waited for some time, knowing that people who live in country houses are often out of them. Mrs. Payne might be out in the garden. It was difficult to guess what, late of a November afternoon, she might be doing in a garden. But still—

Pam put the receiver back, finally. She went back to the fire. She said that, of course, there was no reason really, to suppose that Mrs. Payne had gone back to her house in Ridgefield. She might, of course, have gone anywhere. She might—

Pam went back to the telephone and dialed again, and listened again to distant ringing. Sometimes country people hear a bell ringing from some distance, and hurry in only to be too late.

The telephone was not answered. Pam went back across the room and, midway, felt something which was rather like a physical chill. This time, she did not sit down. She stood in front of the fire, which was now only a nostalgic flicker. But it was not the failure of a needless fire in a warm room which had caused a contracting chill.

"Mrs. Mason," Pam North said, "does he know where they live? Your son, I mean. Where the Paynes live?"

"Why yes," Gladys said. "He was the one who showed me the picture. He said—it doesn't matter, does it, what he said?"

It did not. But that he had known—

"You told him what she said? About seeing someone?"

"Of course. That was what—" She did not finish, but her body stiffened; there was a sudden fixation of the eye muscles, so that her eyes turned starey. And Faith said, *"Oh. He wouldn't—"*

It did not need to be said; it would only hurt to have it said. But it was a chill in the room. A murderer is

136

seen and no good may come to the person who sees him.

"You were to meet him at Grand Central," Pam said. That much had to be said. "Trains run from there to Connecticut. Not to Ridgefield, I don't think, but to somewhere near—near enough."

Mrs. Mason did not say anything. Faith said, "But, dear—" and did not finish.

"He *wouldn't*," Gladys said. "I know he—"

But she stopped with that. She didn't know what the boy would do or wouldn't do. She had told them that already.

11

Bill Weigand parked his car in the upper West Fifties and told the Telegraph Bureau where the car was, and that for some time he wouldn't be in it, and where he would be. He walked a quarter of a block and looked at his destination and involuntarily shook his head.

It had been a very foolish place to build a theater, even in the twenties, when it had seemed that New York could never have enough theaters. Probably it had been a "jinx house" even then, which was only a way of saying that it had been, usually for a few nights at a time, occupied by plays which couldn't find better lodging and that usually because they deserved none. And "The Excelsior" is not really a name anyone in his right mind would wish on a theater.

The name of the theater was still lettered across its façade. It was lettered now in the empty sockets of light bulbs long since shattered. The brick of the façade had once been painted white. That had been a mistake, too.

The theater into which Livingston Birdwood's production of *Uprising,* a play in three acts by Lars Simon, based on a novel by Anthony Payne, was to open during the holidays, was ten blocks south, where theaters belong. It was by no means new—no theater in New York is really new—but it was bright with paint, and lights sparkled on it. It was also occupied by a musical which only now, after rather more than two years, was beginning to dwindle away.

Plays must rehearse somewhere. The Excelsior was a hulk, but it still had a stage of sorts. Electricity could be turned on when needed, and if ancient wiring started fire, those within could always run and the reluctant owners of the building could chortle. The insurance company might sigh, but with resignation, since it had long since got its own back.

From the sidewalk, the theater looked as dead as the empty sockets of its sign. Bill Weigand looked at it and felt doubt; wondered whether, conceivably, Livingston Birdwood had directed him up a blind alley. It was a cobweb of a thought, and he brushed it away and went into the lobby. Plaster had fallen off the lobby ceiling and not been brushed up. There was no one in the lobby. There was no sound except that of his shoes gritting on plaster dust. It was getting on in the day. Perhaps they had packed up and gone home.

The doors from lobby to orchestra were closed against him, flatly, offering no handholds. Gone away and sealed the place up after them? No—a single door with a knob on it. Bill turned the knob and pulled and the door opened, and he went in. They had not packed up and gone home.

The auditorium was not really large. The Excelsior

had been built for "intimate" productions, which had turned out to be intimate to the point of disappearance. But now it looked like a dark cavern—a dark and extremely cold cavern. Bill buttoned his topcoat and resisted the inclination to turn its collar up.

The stage seemed far away, and the center aisle sloped toward it. Over the stage a single bright bulb dangled from a cord, threw down harsh light. In seats nearest the stage half a dozen people sat, dark blobs against the light. Under the hanging light, a man sat on a wooden chair, beside a wooden table, his right leg resting on another wooden chair. Toward the rear of the stage, and to the left as Weigand faced it, a woman in a mink coat stood with her back to him and faced a brick wall.

The man, seen in profile—he was looking at the woman in the mink coat—was young and handsome and dark-haired. A smaller man, whose hair was also dark but was noticeably scant, walked from a canvas flat leaning against a wall (the flat was marked "Laura Darling Scene 2") toward the man in the chair. The walking man said, "Yackety yackety yackety it was you who began it."

The handsome man wheeled quickly to face the newcomer.

"Not I, Sybil," he said, and laughed lightly. "I—"

"Damn it all, Blaine," the smaller man said. "How often do I have to tell you? It's hot as hell. It's got all of you, the heat has. Also, damn it to hell, you've got to start wearing it. Otherwise, you'll be skipping all over the damn place when we open."

"I'm sorry," the handsome man said.

Nobody had paid any attention to Bill Weigand. He sat down in an aisle seat. A broken spring pronged him. He moved to the next seat.

"Blaine." Blaine Smythe. Back in the cast, apparently. Which was mildly interesting, and certainly convenient.

The woman in the mink coat turned. She was pretty, with the highly visible face of an actor.

"Lars," she said. "I still think there ought to be drums. Thump-thump, thump-thump. They're natives, aren't they? I'm looking out this window because I hear the drums—boom-boom-boom, *boom*. I'm scared out of my wits because of the damn drums."

"No drums," Lars—Lars Simon, he would be—said. His tone was weary. "These natives haven't invented drums, darling. Also, they're sneaking up through the jungle. Slither, slither, slither. That's what you hear, darling. Not boom, boom."

"The audience can't hear slither," the girl in mink said. "But it's your play, darling. Slither, slither. God, it's cold in here."

"Button up your overcoat," Lars Simon said, with no sympathy in his voice. "All right. Sybil comes in left." He went back to the flat and then walked away from it, as he had before. "Yackety yackety yackety it was you who began it."

Blaine Smythe seemed to stiffen when he heard the voice. This time he turned slowly, twisting his body but leaving his right leg extended on the chair.

"Not I, Sybil," he said. And laughed lightly. "I—"

The woman in the mink coat turned from the "window." She turned abruptly.

"If not you," she said, "who? That's the question, isn't it, George? Who? If not you—"

"Too fast, darling," Lars Simon said. "Look, darling. The three of you have been cooped up in here for two days, and they're coming through the jungle."

"Slither slither," the girl said.

"You're very funny, darling," Lars said. "You've got on each other's nerves. O.K. But it's hot as hell

141

and you're tired. Beat down. Do it tired, darling. Do it hot."

"With my teeth chattering," the girl said. "Ing gives us a barn to work in and—"

Lars looked at her.

"All right, darling," the girl said. "Cue me, Blaine." She turned and faced the brick wall. Damn it all, Bill Weigand thought, she looks precisely as if she *were* looking out a window. Even under all that coat.

"O.K.," Lars said. "From Sybil's entrance. Yackety yackety yackety it was you who began it."

Blaine Smythe turned even more slowly in his chair. As he turned, he used one hand to lift his right leg a little. He spoke as he turned. "Not I, Sybil. I—"

The young woman turned. Now there was a kind of slump in her slender body, weariness in her slower movement; weariness, yet with hysteria under the weariness, in her voice as she spoke. "If not you," she said, "who? That's the question, isn't it, George? Who—"

She broke. In quite another voice, she said, "Listen, Lars. It's your play. But do you really want me to say 'if not you' again? When it's slowed down this way? To me, darling, it doesn't hold."

Lars Simon said, "Hmmm," thoughtfully and then, "Could be you've got—read it again, darling."

Darling read it again.

Lars nodded. "All right," he said. "Stop with the second 'who.' Only, lean on it a little. Let's take it again. Sybil comes in and yackety yackety yackety—"

They took it again. The girl "leaned" just perceptibly on the second "who."

"O.K.," Lars said. "Faith's cue is the second 'who,' then."

He looked at his watch. "All right, children," he

said. "We've got that in the works. No use trying to set the rest without Faith. Joe?" From some place a man's voice said, "Yeah." "Light this crypt up, will you, Joe?" A few lights came on—two where a cluster once had been; half a dozen dimly outlining the arch. "All right, children," Lars said. "Ten o'clock tomorrow." He came across a runway built over the orchestra pit and down steps. Bill Weigand got up and walked down the center aisle. "And Blaine," Lars Simon said, turning back to the handsome man still sitting by the table. "Tomorrow you bring it along, O.K.? And wear it?"

"Sure," Blaine Smythe said, and stood up. And as he stood, Bill Weigand saw, for the first time, that a rifle was lying across the wooden table. It had been shielded, before, by Blaine Smythe's body.

Smythe moved quickly, with grace, across the stage to the runway. The half dozen dark blobs stood up from their seats and became two women, one middle-aged, the other hardly more than a girl, and four men, one of them a remarkably tall and obviously muscular Negro. "And Tommy," Lars said, "do you mind putting on the choppers, tomorrow? So you can learn to talk with them. And not, buddy, look so goddamn Harvard?"

The tall Negro laughed. He had a low, musical laugh.

"You Amherst boys," he said. He talked Harvard, Weigand thought. "All right, Lars. Tomorrow, ferocious native with pointed teeth. Trouble is, Lars, I bite myself. But—O.K."

Bill Weigand had almost joined the group before anyone seemed to notice him. Then they all turned and looked at him. There was nothing impolite in the way they looked at him. But they looked at an alien.

His identification of himself did not change that, but Blaine Smythe raised his eyebrows, and Lars Simon said, "My God. Who goes willingly?"

Bill Weigand looked as amused as he could manage. He mentioned routine.

"All right," Lars said, "I shot my mouth off. Said he was a pain in the neck and—oh my God, I told somebody he ought to drop dead. I can hear myself. He ought to drop dead, I said. And dead he dropped."

He held out his hands, wrists close enough together. Bill Weigand did not try to look amused. Lars Simon looked at him a moment. "I'm sorry, Captain," he said, in quite another voice. "It isn't funny, is it?"

"No," Bill said. "It's not very funny, Mr. Simon. But it is routine. A couple of questions for you. A couple for—it is Mr. Smythe, isn't it?"

"That's right," Smythe said. He looked at the watch on his wrist. "I have got a date," he said. "Will it take long?"

There was no reason why it should take long. And certainly no reason why the others should wait. The others looked rather as if they'd like to. "Run along, children," Lars Simon said, very much as if he talked to children. They went up the aisle. At the head of it, the young woman in mink stopped and called back. "You really mean *ten,* darling?" she called. "You're damned right, darling," Lars Simon told her up the length of the aisle. "And Tommy. Don't forget the choppers."

"Grrr," Tommy said. He did two steps of what appeared to be a tribal dance.

The three sat in orchestra seats, Simon and Blaine Smythe in one row with a vacant seat between them, Bill Weigand in the row in front, twisted (somewhat uncomfortably) so that he could look at them.

The first was simplest, as it always was. Smythe

had, he said, left the cocktail party shortly after the brawl between Willings and Payne. He had gone to his apartment, which was in the Murray Hill area. He had stayed in it until about seven-thirty, when he had picked up a friend and gone to dinner. "Same friend I've got a date with now," he said, and looked at his watch again. Weigand looked at his own. It showed twenty minutes after four. He said, again, that he'd try not to keep Mr. Smythe long. "Girl friend," Smythe said, without being asked. "They don't like to be kept waiting, Captain."

When it was his turn, Lars Simon was not so quick, nor did he seem so assured. He said that he had still been at the party—what was left of the party. He had not known Payne had been shot until, apparently, about fifteen minutes after it happened. When he had gone out, the police were already there. Somebody had told him Payne was dead, and he had gone home. Home was in Brooklyn Heights.

Probably, while still at the party, he had been with people who would remember that he was with them?

"They'd thinned out, damn it," Simon said. "There was a girl who wants to write plays. There's always somebody who wants to write plays. Wanted to talk about writing plays, for God's sake. I don't know who she was. I don't know when it was. Most of the time I was sitting at a table in a corner having a scotch and writing."

Weigand repeated the last word, his inflection rising.

"Not on paper," Simon said. "In here." He hit his forehead with the palm of his hand. "Second act. Payne had made a hell of a pitch about one scene and I finally said, 'What the hell?' But I still didn't like it and I was trying to work it out so it would make sense and still get by with him. He was a bastard to work with

145

and—" He stopped. He said, "Hell," with considerable simplicity.

"A problem," Weigand said, "which no longer arises, does it?"

"Sure," Lars Simon said. "That's why I killed him, Captain. Terribly sincere artist, that's me. Guy gets in the way of my great art and—poof! No more guy."

"Lars," Blaine Smythe said, and sounded solicitous. "Why be any more of a damn fool than you have to be?"

"He wants motive," Lars Simon said. "I'm the obliging sort. Sincere and obliging. That's me."

"It was that made you say he ought to drop dead?" Bill asked.

"Things like that," Lars said. "All right, he got in my hair." He rubbed his hand hard against his thinning hair, apparently by way of emphasis. "And brother, if I'd killed everybody who got in my hair since I started in this racket—" He spread thin, expressive hands.

"Right," Bill said. "You didn't kill Payne. He annoyed you, but you didn't kill him. You don't know the name of this girl who wants to write plays?"

"No."

"By the way—that rifle." Bill Weigand gestured toward the stage. "It's a working gun?"

"With blanks. It's a prop. Natives closing in on these three, who are all that are left—only they're not, but now it looks that way—and all they've got is this popgun. Natives got the hunting rifles and—" Very evidently he stumbled on sudden realization. "Payne was shot with a rifle?" he said, and no levity was left in his tone.

"A twenty-two," Bill said. He nodded, this time, toward the stage.

"Yes," Lars said. "It's a twenty-two. And so far as I

know it just kicks around here between rehearsals. Joe sees it's on hand when we want—*Joe!*"

A man came from behind a flat, stage right. He said, "Yeah?"

"That damn gun," Lars said, and pointed. "Where do we keep it?"

"With the other props when we get the other props," Joe said. "Which reminds me. About that—"

"Where, Joe?"

"Where it is now, unless we're setting it different. Then—hell, it just gets leaned against a wall, out of the way."

Lars Simon looked at Weigand.

"You've got ammunition for it?" Bill asked, across the orchestra pit.

"Blanks. What the hell?"

Bill said he didn't know what the hell. He told Lars Simon that, for a day or so, they'd have to get along without the rifle. Lars did not seem surprised. He said that, all right, they'd use a broomstick and go "bang!"

"Listen, Captain," Blaine Smythe said. "You don't want me any longer, do you? I've got this—hell, you don't think I'd do anything to good old Tony? And anyway, I wasn't there."

"Right," Bill said. "I understand Mr. Payne got you fired. From this part. Apparently, now he isn't around—"

Blaine said, "Oh, that," in a tone which dismissed that. "He got a bee in his bonnet. Sure. Nothing would have come of it. Look, Captain, you're not that crazy. To get the idea I—hell, man, I could get any one of half a dozen parts. Some of them a helluva lot better, if that's all right with you, Lars."

Lars Simon leaned back slightly and looked at the ceiling far above them. He said, "Sure, Blaine."

"Mr. Smythe," Weigand said, "I understand you and Mrs. Payne—the present Mrs. Payne—are quite good friends."

He was asked what he meant by that. He said he meant no more than he said by that. He said it was a very simple question.

"Listen," Smythe said, "if you mean—"

"No," Bill said. "Only what I said. Asked. Are you?"

Smythe didn't know what he meant by "good." He said they'd met each other around from time to time. He said he'd taken her out a few times. "But that was before she married Payne." He said there had never been anything more than that to it. "Matter of fact," he said, "she's not my type. Probably I'm not her type, either. Anyway, she never acted like it." He looked at Bill Weigand intently. "Somebody tell you different? Or, are you trying a game?"

"No game," Bill said.

"Then?" Smythe said, and once more looked at his watch and, from it, at Weigand, with accusation.

"Go keep your date," Bill said. "If we think of any more questions we'll look you up."

Blaine Smythe stood up quickly. So, not quite so quickly, did Lars Simon.

"Couple more things I'd like to ask you, Mr. Simon," Bill said. "If you haven't got a date too?"

"My wife's used to waiting," Lars Simon said. "Poor wretch."

Bill watched Blaine Smythe, tall and suave of movement, walk up the aisle.

"Mr. Simon," he said, when Smythe had gone out the door, "Payne did get him fired?" Lars nodded. "Why?"

"Thought he knew something about acting," Lars said. "Payne did. Said Blaine didn't 'feel' the part.

148

Feel, for God's sake. Went over my head to Birdy. Ing Birdwood. He had money in it, you know. Payne had. Or maybe Lauren had. You knew she's got money?"

"Yes."

"So Birdy gave Blaine notice. Can at this stage, you know."

"So now he's got the part back?"

"That's right. Now he's got the part back. He's good, as a matter of fact."

"Good enough to have half a dozen other parts for the taking?"

"Captain," Lars said, "they all talk that way, the poor bastards."

"He didn't have?"

"I don't know he didn't have," Lars said. "Of course, the season's moving along. This time of year, things are pretty much set. Off Broadway's another matter. Could be off Broadway. Only, Blaine isn't exactly an art-for-art's-sake sort of bloke. Or Equity-minimum-for-art's-sake either." He looked at Bill Weigand with enhanced interest. He said, "You figure a bloke would kill another bloke for a job?"

Bill said nobody could tell what a bloke would kill another bloke for. He said that if reason entered into murder, there would be no murder. He said, "You don't want to gossip, I suppose? I can't insist if you don't."

"About what?"

"You heard what I asked Smythe."

Lars Simon considered. In due time he nodded his head slowly. He stopped nodding his head, and looked at the stage, where there was, at the moment, nothing worth looking at.

"No," Lars said, "I guess I don't, Captain," and then looked at Bill. "Which," he said, "I suppose you'll take as an answer." Bill said nothing. "I will say this," Lars said. "From what I hear, Tony Payne was a bit of a heel where women were concerned. So if Lauren, who's a nice girl from what I've seen of her—" He let it hang there, for the moment. Then he said, "Payne had latched onto a babe. A chick—a very downy chick. But I suppose you've turned that up?"

"Right," Bill said. "One, anyway. I suppose you mean Jo-An Rhodes?"

"Don't know her name, actually. Pretty little dark thing. Saw them together once or twice and Payne looked—well, you know how men look sometimes. As if he were about to—absorb her. Could be she had a boy friend. Looked the type that would, if boys are what they ought to be." He looked at the stage again. "I don't argue all of them are," he said, rather absently.

People rather kept pointing at Jo-An Rhodes and, by indirection, James Self. In murder investigations, people are rather inclined to point—to point away. Sometimes, of course, merely wishing to be helpful.

"This rifle of yours," Bill said, and Lars shook his head and said, "Not mine. Birdy's."

"Right," Bill said. "This prop rifle. Anyone, obviously—any member of the cast, anybody associated with the production—could walk in and pick it up. Take it anywhere and use it. Get it back for the next day's rehearsal."

"As you say. Obviously. But as far as that goes, anybody, in the cast or not, could walk in and pick it up and, as you say, use it."

"The theater's not kept locked?"

"If you call this barn a theater—no. With what? Nothing works. Why? There's nothing worth stealing."

"The rifle. And anybody who knew it was here, lying around loose, could have told anybody else."

Lars supposed so. Then, somewhat belatedly, the idea seemed to cheer him.

"And this anybody could walk in any time," he said. "As you did yourself, Captain."

There was no special point that Bill could see in their continuing to agree with each other about the rifle.

"When I came in," he said, "you were cueing Smythe. But I gather you're not really playing the part?"

Lars Simon laughed. He said, "My God no. I was standing in for Faith. Faith Constable."

"Who had the day off?"

That was not it. Faith Constable did not have the day off. None of the boys and girls got days off. Not at this stage. Faith had showed with the others. "She's a trouper, the Lady Constable." But, an hour or so after she had arrived, she had got a telephone call. "Believe it or not, we've got a telephone in this dump." She had told Lars that something had come up, and that he would have to get along without her for the afternoon. She had not said what had come up. Lars had raised no objection. "You don't with La Constable. She knows who she is. In a nice way, but she knows who she is."

Simon had no idea—no idea at all—what had suddenly "come up"?

He had not. It was clear, however, that it was something Faith Constable thought important. "As I said, she's a trouper."

A detective, mind concentrated on a case, risks obsession. There was no reason to suppose, Bill told himself, that what had seemed "important" to Mrs. Faith Constable had any relation to what was, at the moment, most important to Homicide, Manhattan West. All sudden and unexplained movements are, however, interesting.

As a matter of routine, no one else in the case bore a grudge against Anthony Payne? Nobody Lars Simon knew of?

Lars considered briefly. It was a hell of a big cast. The ones Weigand had seen were only principals. There were a lot of walk-ons, mostly natives.

"Payne did have a habit—bad habit—of treating Tommy as if he were a native," Lars said. "You saw Tommy? Harvard '56, cum laude. I don't imagine it bothered Tommy. He's the most goddamn well-adjusted bloke I ever saw." He considered again. "Among actors, anyway," he said.

"Mr. Payne has been attending rehearsals?"

Lars rubbed his receding hair with both hands, in apparent anguish. He said, "And how!" He turned to Bill Weigand. "Do you really have to catch the bloke who spared us Payne?" he said.

Bill said he had to try, and went across the runway over the orchestra pit and got the rifle. There was no point in bothering about any fingerprints which might be on it. If it had a story to tell, its grooves would speak mutely. Ballistics would decipher the word.

In his car, Bill Weigand call the Telegraph Bureau to see whether anybody wanted him. Nobody did. With the motor started, Bill wrestled briefly with temptation. He might now go home, where Dorian was waiting. He might, showered and changed, with her beside him, drive across town and downtown and have with Pam and Jerry North the drink to which they had been invited. The temptation was considerable.

In the back seat of the car there was a rifle which might—and of course might not—prove to be a State exhibit. And, above the soft sound of the Buick's motor, he could hear a voice—a legal voice. "Now, Captain," the voice said to an inner ear, "you found this rifle, you say. And you took it at once to the office, of course, and marked it properly and dispatched it, as is required in the regulations of the department, for ballistic examination? Oh—you didn't do that? You took it home with you? Up to your apartment? Is that right? And then you and your wife went to the apartment of Mr. and Mrs.—let's see, now. North, isn't it?—and still had the rifle with you? Carried it around quite a time, didn't you, Captain? You're sure that there was no opportunity for somebody to substitute another rifle for the one you say you found in the theater? That's what you say, Captain? Remembering you are on oath. You expect this jury to—"

Bill Weigand, who was only a few crosstown blocks from his apartment which overlooks the East River, drove downtown to West Twentieth Street, and carried the rifle upstairs, and put a tag on it and initialed the tag, and called for a patrolman to take it to ballistics. The patrolman gave him a receipt for it, and put his own initials under Weigand's on the tag, and took the rifle downstairs again to a police car and drove off with it.

The telephone on Bill's desk rang. Connecticut State Police, Ridgefield Barracks. Reporting: Mrs. Anthony Payne had returned to her house on Nod Road. She had returned alone at a little before five. The State Police had been keeping an eye on the house at the request of Anthony Payne who, some days before, had told them that the house would be empty, that he and his wife would be in New York and that the couple who constituted the staff had been given the time off. At a little before five, the eyes being kept—those of Trooper Owen Cutler—had seen lights go on in the house. To verify, he had driven up to it and found Mrs. Payne there, alone. (Alone by her statement; he had not, of course, searched.) He had expressed sympathy, been thanked, driven off. Did Captain Weigand want any further steps taken?

Bill hesitated. He could not think of any. But still— Would they mind keeping an eye on the house, as manpower permitted? Not that anything would happen. But still—

The State Police said, "O.K., Captain."

So—it was still not much after five. Bill checked through his mind. He found a nagging in his mind. There is always something and what now was this— this vague and unsatisfactory thing; this kind of scratching, as if something shut out sought admittance or something inside wanted out? Something he had passed over which should not have been passed over, and which now was scratching his subconscious? Weigand flipped the mental pages of the day, and turned up nothing. Well, if it was important, it would nag, would tickle, its way to the surface. Meanwhile—

The telephone rang. A young woman was at the desk downstairs and wanted to see Captain Weigand. Young woman named Jo-An Rhodes. Did Weigand want—?

12

There is a Navy injunction which has to do with the dignity of the service. In one variant, it goes: "A Naval officer never drinks. But if he drinks he never gets drunk. But if he gets drunk he never falls down. But if he falls down he falls on his stripes."

Excessive drinking is not a problem to Pamela North. But she has problems of her own. She has an injunction for herself, and it goes: "Don't stick your neck out. But if you stick your neck out, tell somebody you're going to. But if you don't tell somebody you're going to, have a convincing reason for not telling. But if your reason would not convince most people, be sure that it convinces you."

When she and Faith Constable had made their minds up, and made Gladys Mason's up for her, there was a self-convincing reason not to tell the police—not even Bill Weigand—what they were about to be up to. The whole point was to reach a frightened boy, give a frightened boy a chance to explain; reach him before there was too much to explain. It was, admittedly, the taking of a chance, conceivably a chance with a woman's life. "He won't," Mrs. Mason said. "I know he won't." Which was something, if not enough. The main point was more simple: If the boy planned to do anything, he had already had all afternoon to do it in.

But to tell Jerry was an entirely different matter. He would, Pam realized, kick and scream. After kicking, he would put his foot down. But in the end, he might even come with them, which would be satisfactory—very satisfactory indeed.

From the telephone in the shadows of Faith Constable's apartment, Pam dialed Jerry's office; asked to speak to Jerry, listened and said, in a diminished tone, "Oh."

Jerry was with author, business consultation over a drink or two; precise whereabouts unknown. Being a publisher, Pam often thinks, requires a good deal of drinking. He was expected back at the office.

"Well," Pam said, "when he gets back, tell him—no, I'll dictate it."

The girl still wore the shapeless sweater and tweed skirt, but now with a topcoat over them. She wore brown oxfords, a little scuffed. Her short dark hair looked as if wind had blown it. Standing in the doorway to Bill Weigand's office, looking up at him from large dark eyes, she might almost have been a schoolgirl. One rather expected to see books under one arm, perhaps with a strap around them.

Bill said, "Come in, Miss Rhodes."

When she moved she was not a schoolgirl. No looseness of sweater, bulk of skirt, could wholly blur the slender grace of body, the subtlety of movement. Most schoolgirls move like colts; the lucky ones like kittens.

She moved a few steps toward the desk Bill Weigand stood behind and stopped, and looked up at him with strange, obviously unhappy, intensity. It was as if she had asked a question, waited desperately for an answer. Something's the matter with the kid, Bill thought. What ails the kid?

"You've arrested him," Jo-An Rhodes said. "Locked him up somewhere. And he hasn't done anything. Not anything."

Her voice was angry; her voice accused.

"It isn't fair," she said. "He's—he's not the way you think he is."

Bill shook his head slowly. He said, "Sit down, won't you?" and indicated the chair at the end of his desk. She paid no attention to that. "I'm afraid," he said, "I don't know what you're talking about, Miss Rhodes. Arrested whom?"

He saw that, when she was not speaking, the girl's lips trembled. Full lips, softly curved—trembling lips.

"There's no use lying about it," she said. "I'll get a lawyer. You can't just lock him up. Incommunicado."

Bill felt himself blink at the word. It sounded, on her lips, like a word she had read somewhere. It occurred to him that her mind—her young mind—was now a restless amalgam of what she had read, what in her few years encountered.

"No," he said, and smiled at her. "I'm not lying. And we don't hold people incommunicado. Against the law that is, Miss Rhodes." His tone put quotation marks around the long word.

Her face was very white. She shook her head slowly, but now not with assurance.

"Who do you think we've arrested?" Bill asked her. And then, again, asked her why she didn't sit down. She did sit down, then. She wore short white socks on bare legs. Again she was like a schoolgirl—a schoolgirl very lucky with her legs.

"Who?" Bill said once more.

She looked at him long and carefully before she answered, obviously studying his face.

"Jim," she said. "Jim Self. Where is he, then? What's happened to him?"

"Has something happened to him?"

She nodded her head.

"He's so sure," she said, "about everything. Ideas and—and everything. He's brilliant. You could see that this morning. Couldn't you see that?"

She seemed actually to expect an answer.

"Right," Bill said. "But—the point is—"

"But he orders too many books because they're good and people ought to buy them," she said. "Things like that. Practical things. He calls me 'child' and 'baby.' All right. Only, I know all that. What I am. But, some ways, I'm older than he'll ever be."

Almost any woman's comment on almost any man, Bill thought. Made with most assurance by a beginning woman, like this pretty girl. Sometimes trues and sometimes not. At the moment, certainly not germane.

"I take it," Bill said, "Mr. Self has—gone some place? He's not here. You can take my word for that. Not arrested. Why did you think he had been arrested?"

Again she looked at him, studied him. She said, "You don't think he killed Mr. Payne?"

"We don't know who killed Mr. Payne," he told her, his tone patient. "We haven't arrested anybody. Why would he want to kill Mr. Payne?"

"No reason," she said. "But—oh, it was clear enough what you thought. You don't have to believe what I told you about Mr. Payne and me. It was true, but that doesn't matter. To Jim I'm just—just a girl who works in the shop. Just anybody. Nobody at all."

She wanted him to believe that. That was evident. Whether she believed it herself—wanted to believe it—Germane enough, perhaps. Too elusive, obviously, for the moment.

"So he wouldn't have any reason. Can't you see that?"

"All right," Bill said. "Say I do see that. And—suppose you tell me what this is all about. Mr. Self has—what? Failed to show up somewhere?"

"At the shop. To be there, really. You see—"

This was Wednesday. On Wednesday evenings, the bookshop was kept open until ten o'clock. As a result, there was a routine.

Jo-An opened the shop at ten in the morning. Some time between twelve and one, Self relieved her. As he had today.

"You mentioned an auction," Bill said.

She made a small gesture. "I thought maybe you'd go," she said. "It was—all right, it was silly."

She looked at him.

"Right," Bill said. "Go ahead. He came. We had our little talk. Then?"

Then, as on any other Wednesday, she had left the shop, and James Self to run it. She was, according to Wednesday routine, due back at around five, to mind the store for two hours. At seven, or thereabouts, Self returned and she went home, or wherever she wanted to go. That was the Wednesday routine. But today, something had happened to the routine.

She had gone as usual. She had returned at around five, perhaps a few minutes after five—"about half an hour ago"—and found the shop closed. Closed and dark. She had let herself in, and found the shop empty. She had looked for a message, and found none.

"I suppose," she said, "you'll think this is all—all nothing. That something came up—some trivial thing—and he closed up and—" She shook her head.

"It isn't like him," she said. "Maybe that doesn't sound like anything either. But it isn't like him."

People do move in patterns. They do what it is "like" them to do. If this pretty child felt it was not "like" Self to close up shop, to go off without explanation, she was quite probably right.

"Right," Bill said. "It sounds like something. A dozen explanations—a hundred. But I agree some explanation is needed. So?"

She had been worried. "Everything's worrying now," she said, with a kind of resentment. She had turned on the lights and waited for a few minutes, and then got it into her head that "Jim was sick. Maybe up in his apartment all alone."

She had locked the shop up again, and gone up to Self's apartment on the third floor in the same building. She had knocked and then called and then gone in.

"His apartment wasn't locked?"

She appeared to be surprised. She said, "Of course it was locked. I don't—oh. The key to the shop unlocks his apartment. He hates to be bothered with a lot of keys. When he rented the shop and the apartment, he had the same locks put on both."

Again she looked at Bill, and now as if for a signal. He said, "Go ahead."

"That's all, really," she said. "He wasn't there and then, all at once, I knew. He'd been arrested. You'd arrested him. I called and they told me where you'd be and—and so I came. But you say he isn't—"

For the first time, her voice faltered. And, suddenly, her dark eyes went under the water of her tears.

"Where is he?" she said, and her young voice

shook. "I was so sure. But now—*what's happened to him?*"

Bill was patient. Probably nothing had happened to James Self. Probably something quite trivial had come up, made it necessary for him to leave the shop.

"Without leaving me a note or anything?"

There was, of course, that. But probably he had expected to be back before she came.

"By the way," Bill said. "When you were in his apartment, did you notice anything? I mean—anything to show he might have taken things with him. Clothes—a suitcase—"

She shook her head. She said, "I didn't—pry. I wouldn't. Anyway—I wouldn't have been able to tell, would I?"

The question was innocent; it implied innocence. Not that Bill had much doubted that Self occupied the apartment alone. "Not with Miss Rhodes." Still, all things must be somewhat doubted.

"As a matter of fact," Bill said, "it's quite in the cards he's got back to the shop. Probably wondering right now where you are. Wait a minute—what's the number of the shop?"

She gave him the telephone number of James Self, Books. He gave it to the switchboard and waited. The telephone in the shop rang unanswered. While he waited, she looked up at him, eyes wide, eyes hopeful. The hope faded slowly from the wet eyes.

"Not yet, apparently," Bill said. "But that's still the most likely thing. Probably by the time you get there, he'll be there waiting."

"You really think that?"

"Right. Anyway, I think it's the most likely. Of course, if he doesn't show up in an hour or so—well, if he doesn't, call back. If I'm not here, I'll leave word and we'll start things moving. All right?"

He felt somewhat like a doctor, giving an encouraging prognosis. No use scaring a patient, even when you're not so sure.

Moderate hope seemed to return to the girl's dark eyes. She stood up.

"If he doesn't come you'll—help?"

"Of course."

"I really did think you'd arrested him. Weren't—weren't letting anybody know. Maybe were doing something to make him talk."

Bill stood up. He shook his head and smiled down at her.

"I'm sorry," she said. "If—if he doesn't show up and I call here—there'll be somebody who'll know what I'm talking about?"

"Right. If I'm not here."

She went toward the door; was opening it when Bill thought of something. Had James Self a car? If he had, where did he keep it?

He had; she told him where and turned and said, her voice again a little tremulous, "You think—?"

"Nothing. Just an easy thing to check up on. Probably he's wondering where on earth you've got to. Next thing we know, he'll come rushing in, thinking we've arrested *you*."

She smiled very faintly. "I don't think he worries about me that much," she said. "Good night, Captain."

Perhaps, Bill thought, Self will be at the shop, waiting. It *is* the most likely thing. Of course, as had been true of Faith Constable, sudden and unexplained movement is always interesting.

He rang and garage Jo-An had named. It was some time before the telephone was answered, and the voice was grumpy.

Self kept a car there—a 1956 Chevrolet. He had

picked it up an hour or so ago and driven off in it. Bill said, "Thanks."

Was Self running? It would be very helpful if he were. But nobody was chasing him. Not yet, anyway. And not time to start yet.

Bill Weigand was opening the door between his office and the squad room when the telephone rang behind him. Alexander Graham Bell really loused things up, Bill thought, and went back to stop the insistent bell.

First they had gone over a manuscript, in Jerry's office. It was a long manuscript, and going over it had taken some time. To whom was this pronoun relative? Was this a typo, or something intended? If intended, what was it supposed to mean? Granted that past-participial construction is sometimes desirable, even necessary, couldn't it, on pages 223 to 226 be squirmed out of sooner? The author said, "hmmm-m," to that and read pages 223 to 226. "Do rather drag hads after me, don't I?" he said. "Clang a bit, don't they?" He made changes. Step by step they reached the end on page 334. The author said, "We've earned a drink." They went for a drink, Jerry promising to return to the office, saying he might be late, assuring Miss Arby he need not be waited for and that he would sign the letters and drop them down the chute himself.

Miss Arby, who was briskly efficient, rather new on the staff, and had had considerable experience with employers, looked doubtful.

"I'm quite up to it," Jerry told her, gravely, and she said, "Oh, Mr. *North*," and flushed. He grinned at her; efficient secretaries are not easy to come by. She realized it was time to laugh, and laughed.

Drinks seldom are singular, particularly when publishers drink with authors, publishers—one immemorial tradition of which all authors approve—paying. This author proved only reasonably thirsty, but was loquacious. Authors who have finally shrugged away a pack shouldered for many months often are.

It was getting on for six when Jerry let himself into his dark office and switched on lights. The staff, as directed, had not waited for him. On his desk, half a dozen letters, one filled-in contract, awaited him, a stamped envelope clipped to each. He read; he signed; he folded and sealed up. The contract was on the bottom, and took a little longer; was signed in triplicate and put in envelope. Enough postage? There appeared to be, and Miss Arby would not make a mistake. She made few. So, that finished and—

It was not finished. Underneath the contract, visible now, was an interoffice memo, for the attention of Mr. North. It was neatly typed—all Miss Arby's typing was neat. It read:

"Mrs. North called 4:53 and dictated following:

" 'Have to go to Ridgefield, Conn., with Mrs. Constable. See Mrs. Payne. Have Martha fix you something. I'll drive carefully. If I'm late, tell Bill there's something the matter with his legs.' "

Jerry read this three times, running fingers anxiously through his hair. He is used to Pam's being up to something, and used to her being cryptic about it, commonly with no such intention. But this time she had him stumped. On the third reading, he began to be uneasily suspicious that stumping was what she had intended. And this was not in the least like Pamela North.

A call for help? A warning? An effort to suggest without revealing? If so, a failure, unless Pam had intended to suggest that she had taken leave of her senses. Wait—listened to while she telephoned, veiling her meaning from alien ears? Suddenly, Jerry North felt the inner tightness of anxiety. "I wish to God," Jerry North said, speaking aloud in an empty office, "you wouldn't do this sort of thing to me, Pam. Pam girl—I wish—"

He heard his voice in the empty office. He was slightly embarrassed, but no less anxious. He dialed a number he did not need to look up, and waited. He said, "Captain Weigand, please," and tried to keep anxiety out of his voice. He said, "Bill? Do you know what Pam's up to?"

Bill said, "Hi, Jerry. What?"

"What Pam's up to. She's left the damnedest message and, apparently, gone to Ridgefield with Faith Constable. Listen—"

Bill Weigand listened. As a result, he felt somewhat dazed. He said, "Read it again, will you?" and listened while it was read again.

"Is there," Jerry said, "something the matter with your legs? Something you need to be told about?"

"It doesn't make sense," Bill said. "As for my legs, no. I—you're sure it says *my* legs?"

"You heard it," Jerry said. " 'Tell Bill there's something the matter with his legs.' "

"Your girl must have got it wrong."

"My girl," Jerry said, "is efficient. She is of a practical turn of mind. She thinks in simple declarative sentences. This, on the other hand, is Pam. Pure Pam. Only more than usual. Do you suppose there was some reason she couldn't say what she wanted to? I thought perhaps—"

He told Bill his theory that Pam might have been being listened to. He said, "Look. If anything happens to Pam—"

"Take it easy," Bill said. "Nothing ever does, really."

"The hell it doesn't. She's got herself into more—"

"I said 'really,' " Bill told him. "Hold it a minute, won't you?"

Jerry held it a minute.

"You don't," Bill said, "tell somebody there's something the matter with his legs. If there's something the matter—"

"Of course," Jerry said. "It's one of those damned relatives. "I've been up to my ears in them most of the—"

"Huh?"

"Relative pronouns," Jerry said. "Never mind about my ears. The legs aren't yours. They're somebody else's. As in, 'I saw John Smith this afternoon. Tell Bill there's something the matter with his legs.' Probably that's what Pam thought she had said."

Jerry became conscious of a kind of absence at the other end of the telephone wire. He waited and the absence continued. He said, "Bill?"

"Let me think, will you?"

"By all means," Jerry said, and waited.

"I thought I had something," Bill said. "It's slipped out of reach. As for your sentences—why not, 'I saw the man who killed Payne'? And then the business about the legs?"

Jerry North said, "Damn," and heard his own voice go up. "Oh damn it." He stopped himself, breathed deeply. "You mean," he said, and spoke very carefully, "Pam found out who killed Payne? And—*that he was the one listening when she phoned me?*"

"Take it easy."

"If it were Dorian you'd—"

"I said, take it easy. If it had been the murderer, she'd hardly have mentioned his legs in front of him, would she? Not Pam. Wait—Lauren Payne had a front room at the hotel. Apparently she was in it—left the party early. If she had been looking out the window—

if our man had been going into the hotel across the street—a man with something wrong with his legs—a man she knew, and a man with something against her husband— *Wait!* She went to see Pam this morning. Wanted to find out whether she'd said anything. Perhaps she had. Perhaps Pam remembered. Perhaps—"

"The hell with perhaps," Jerry said. "All right. Grant them all. She's gone up there. Into—into what, Bill? I'm not going to sit around and—wait while you think. I'm—"

"For God's sake," Bill said. "Get hold of yourself, Jerry. Nobody's going to sit around. I'll pick you up and we'll go have a look-see."

"And meanwhile?"

"Meanwhile," Bill said, "the State cops are keeping an eye on things. Simmer down, my friend."

Bill put the telephone back in its cradle and sat for a moment looking at it. Then he got up and walked to the door of his office and opened it and looked into the squad room. Mullins was still there.

"Sergeant," Bill Weigand said, "there's something I wish you'd do. Shouldn't take you too long. I'm going up to the Payne house with Jerry North. So if you'll—"

State Trooper Cutler had backed his car off the road onto what had once been a cowtrack, providing footing between fenced field and road. It had been years since cows had trod it, but it was still firm, and a place to make a car inconspicuous. From the car, Cutler could see the Payne house on a hill opposite. It was lighted up. Pretty house. Cutler wouldn't want to spend a winter there. Not with all that glass. But probably the Paynes hadn't needed to. Probably they'd gone to Florida or somewhere in the winter.

Somewhere warm. His radio squawked. It said, "Car Twelve. Calling Car Twelve."

Cutler picked the receiver up, switched over, said, "Car Twelve."

"Where are you?"

"Stake-out on Payne house. Nothing happening and—"

"Three-car smashup on Seven above Branchville. Sounds like a bad one, Owney. Get going, huh?"

Trooper Owen Cutler said, "Will do." And did.

13

The reflectors in a sign picked up the car lights, spelled out a name: "Payne." Pam turned the car off the narrow blacktop, sharply up a graveled drive. The drive stretched more than two hundred yards ahead; it climbed and curved gently. The long low house was a long band of light on top the ridge. It seemed to float there.

Pam drove fast on the drive, urging the car. For the last few miles a sense of urgency had held her. Faith Constable, sitting beside Pam, had leaned forward, as if to speed the car. In the back seat, a dark shadow among shadows, Gladys Mason had sat quietly. Since they had stopped for directions at the drugstore, the mother of the boy they were trying to find had seemed to hide inside herself.

They had taken the Norths' car because it was the only one—unless, as Faith had uncertainly suggested, they wanted to hire a Carey car, with a man to drive it. There had been no point in that, Pam had said. "Cum-

bersome," she said. "What would we do with him?"
They had had no difficulty—except the difficulties of
darkness, toward the end of narrow, winding roads—
in reaching Ridgefield. That far Pam—because Jerry
had an author living in Redding and they had been to
her house—knew her way. But when they reached a
fountain on Route 35—a fountain sheathed, for the
winter—what they next did was anybody's guess. Pam
turned left, driving toward lights up Ridgefield's Main
Street.

It was almost seven o'clock by then and most of
Main Street appeared to have gone to bed. In the
unassertive stores on Main Street, a street on which
once had thudded the heavy feet of British soldiers,
marching down from the burning of Danbury, night
lights burned dimly. Except for a news store, except
for a drugstore. Pam tried the drugstore.

The soda clerk knew where the Paynes lived. "Awful thing about poor Mr. Payne." Pam was headed the
wrong way. Turn—all right to U-turn at the traffic
light, in a lane between parked cars—and drive two
blocks or so to Branchville Road. Had a number—
Route 102. Mile or so on it and, to the right, Nod
Road. No number. Couple of miles more on Nod
Road, beyond Whipstick Road, and the Payne house
was a couple of hundred yards back, on the left—
about three miles altogether. "You can't miss it," the
soda clerk said, with confidence. Pam was less certain;
even after she had got it repeated, committed to memory, she was not certain. Whipstick Road probably
would throw her off; it sounded like a road which
might.

"Can't miss it," the soda clerk repeated, firmly. "Like I told the other two."

Pam had turned to go back to the car. She stopped.
She said, "The other two?"

"Like you, miss," the soda clerk said. "She needs people to stand by time like this. Tough to be out there all alone. At a time like this."

"Yes," Pam said. "Other friends of hers, of course. Men? Or women?"

Both the others who had asked had been men. The most recent, about half an hour ago. Tall guy. Dark. Had a car outside. "Course, I don't know. There could have been a lady in the car." He had, with proper impartiality, told him what he had told Pam, how to get to Nod Road. The man had gone out to the car and driven off.

The other had been earlier. Also a tall guy—tall and thin; younger, he thought, than the second enquirer. He had come in about two, or a little after. "Right after the bus stopped. Bus from New York." He might have come on the bus. On the other hand, he'd probably had a car. Most people had cars, didn't they? Hard to find a place to park at that earlier hour. Shoppers.

"Did you happen to notice," Pam said, "whether either of them limped?"

The soda clerk put his head back and closed his eyes, in the attitude of one deep in remembrance. He opened his eyes and adjusted his head and said, "Can't remember that either of them did. But I didn't pay much attention. Pretty busy the first time and a lot of the kids at the counter the second. Neither of them was what I'd call crippled, if you know what I mean. But whether they limped—" He shrugged to end the sentence.

Either, but most probably the first, might have been Robert Mason, seeking to close a dangerous mouth. Pam had told the two women in the car and Mrs. Mason had drawn a slow, shuddering breath and gone back into herself. "Hours ago," Faith Constable said. "He may—" She did not finish.

"We came as fast as we could," Pam said. "As soon as we—as we had reason."

She swung the car from the curb, U-turned at the light. She drove faster than she should on a village street; on Branchville Road faster still, although Branchville Road is curving, not wide. She almost missed Nod Road and had to back to turn into it. It had, hurrying on a still narrower road, lights boring into darkness under arching trees, seemed farther than the man had said. But, finally, the car lights picked up the sign. Gravel spurted under rear wheels as Pam sent the car up the drive. Near the house, the drive went through a gap in a thick hedge. That was why, from below, the house had seemed to float. It floated above the hedge.

There was no other car on the drive, which looped in front of the long house—a house which, as they stopped in front of it, seemed all glass. A porch roof, cantilevered over a terrace, seemed to be tipping a hat to them.

Pam was first out of the car, but had to go around it. By the time she reached the terrace, Faith Constable was holding the rear door open. Mrs. Mason got out of the car slowly, as if she dreaded to leave the car—the safe shadows of the car.

They were only halfway across the wide terrace when the door onto it opened. Lauren Payne stood with the light behind her, her coppery hair shining in the light. A black dress hugged her slender body. She stood so for a moment, light-outlined, and then said, in her low, husky voice, "Why—hello."

It had seemed, when she opened the door, that she expected them; it had been almost as if they were invited guests, a little behind their time. But when she spoke, she spoke with surprise. But then, a little vaguely, she said, "Why, how nice. Faith dear. Mrs. North." She looked at Gladys Mason, her smile one of uncertainty.

"You're all right?" Pam said, and Lauren looked at her for a second, as if puzzled, and then said, "All right?"

It had been, Pam thought, a strange thing to ask a woman violently widowed only twenty-four hours before.

"Why yes," Lauren said, "I'm all right, I guess."

She drew back from the door and said, "Come in."

They went in.

"This is Gladys Mason, dear," Faith said. "She's—" She hesitated.

"I was Tony's second wife," Gladys said, and her voice was dull. "A long time ago."

She looked around the room, as if her eyes sought something.

It was a long room, two sides of glass. There was a big fireplace in one wall, and a fire laid in it, but not lighted. There was no place in the room for a man to hide, or for a frightened, angry boy to hide.

"Do come and sit down," Lauren said, and led them down the room to chairs near the fireplace. Then she shivered a little, and said, "Wait," opened a narrow door in the wall near the fireplace and took out a foot-long, narrow box. She got a very long wooden match from the box and struck it and leaned down and touched the little flame to paper under wood. A larger flame leaped up. "Do sit down," she said, again, and they sat down. But after a moment, Lauren stood up again and walked to the glass which faced the terrace and looked through it. She came back. "I thought I saw somebody coming," she said.

A car's lights, Pam thought, would be brightly visible as a car came up the drive, at least until the hedge intervened. The lights would hardly be something one "thought" one saw.

"We shouldn't just have—barged in this way," Pam said. "Probably you're expecting—"

"Nobody," Lauren said, quickly, in the voice too deep for so slight a woman. "It was good of you to come. I must get you something. I'm sorry—I'm not thinking very clearly, I'm afraid. I'll—"

She started to move away, apparently to get them something.

"Dear," Faith Constable said, "we came because—"

But Gladys Mason interrupted her. The woman in dull clothes spoke in a dull voice.

"Mrs. Payne" she said, "did you see my boy? Was that what you meant?"

Lauren turned back. She said, "See your boy? What do you mean, Mrs.—" she hesitated over the name, came up with it. "Your boy?"

"Robert," Gladys Mason said. "He—he was a bus at the hotel. A tall, thin boy. Dark. Is he the one you meant?"

"I'm afraid—" Lauren said, and came back to her chair by the fire. "Should I know what you're talking about, Mrs. Mason?"

"The boy," Gladys said, and there was no change in her voice—she spoke methodically, with almost no inflection. "You don't remember?"

"We weren't at the hotel long," Lauren said. "You mean the Dumont? We didn't eat there. Tony said the food was terrible. He was like that about—things."

"Not then," Gladys said, and now there was a little impatience in her voice. "That's not what I'm talking about. Mrs. Payne, don't you remember me?"

"Remember? I knew there was—that Tony married

someone after Faith, before me. Is that what you mean? Did we meet sometime? I'm terribly sorry. I don't remember. I'm so dreadfully bad at—"

Gladys Mason shook her head.

"I don't mean that," she said. "Last night. After—after Tony was shot. After Mrs. North told you and—"

"I remember Mrs.-North—coming," Lauren said. Then she said, "*Wait!* Of course I remember you. It's—it's all been so—so like a dream. I keep forgetting things. You came and sat with me after the doctor gave me something to make me sleep. Somebody said, 'This is Mrs. Mason. She'll stay with you for a little.' " She shook her head slowly. "It was dreadful of me to forget," she said. "I've been—nothing has seemed quite real. I'm—it was good of you to sit with me."

She looked suddenly at Mrs. North and then, her eyes a little widened, again at Gladys Mason. Whatever she had forgotten, Pam thought, she remembered clearly enough now.

"But," Lauren said, her deep voice very low indeed, "after you came I must have passed out. Passed out like a light, as they say. I remember your coming in and now somebody saying your name and I said, 'a nurse?' Didn't I? And somebody said, 'the housekeeper.' Wasn't that it?"

"Not all of—" Gladys said, and Lauren leaned forward in her chair and, again, said, "Wait. Please—did I say something to you? Something about your boy? But—how could I? I—I'm sorry, Mrs. Mason. I don't know anything about your boy. Not even that you and Anthony had a son. Not his name. Not anything." She looked very intently at Mrs. Mason. "You say 'what I meant.' Do you mean I did say something?" Then she looked quickly at Pam North.

"No," Pam said. "Not to me. I told you that. But, to her—"

"You said," Gladys Mason told the woman with coppery hair, who sat beside the fire, light from above touching her hair, "that he was not supposed to be over there. Your voice wasn't clear, but you said that. It was as if you were talking in your sleep."

"I don't remember. I don't know what I meant. Certainly nothing about your—"

"I asked you what you meant by 'over there' and you said, 'The King Arthur, of course.' That's the hotel across the street. You said 'he' didn't belong over there. 'What's he doing over there?'"

Lauren shook her head again.

"Maybe I did," she said. "I don't remember. If I did, I don't know what I meant. Not belonging at the King Arthur? But—it's just a hotel. Anybody can 'belong' at a hotel."

"Not," Gladys said, "a busboy who works at a hotel across the street. Oh—I don't say it's clear. But—did you see him? Or—was it somebody else? Going into the other hotel. Your husband could have been shot from there."

"See somebody?" She shook her head again. "I don't understand—" She looked toward Pam, then toward Faith Constable. "Can't one of you," she said, "tell me what this is all about? Why you've come here to—to ask these questions?"

"At the Dumont," Pam said, "your windows faced the street. You could look across at the King Arthur. Mrs. Mason thinks you did, and saw her son going in. You see, she's afraid. The boy hated his father because—oh, for lots of reasons. He may have had a rifle."

"But—" Lauren said.

"You said," Gladys told her, "that there was something the matter with his leg. The man, whoever it was, you saw. And—Bobby limps. Not all the time. When he's tired and—"

"Listen," Lauren said. "Will you—will all of you—listen to me a minute? I didn't see anybody. I don't really know what you're talking about. I suppose—all right. I'm not questioning what you say, Mrs. Mason. I said some things when I was—well, when I was drugged. I don't remember. What you say I said doesn't make any sense to me now. But whatever it was, it couldn't have had anything to do with what happened to Tony. Because—"

She paused and partly closed her eyes. She was, Pam thought, arranging what she wanted to say, getting it clear in her own mind.

"I suppose," she said, and spoke slowly, as if she thought of each word, was still working it out as she spoke. "I suppose if I had seen anybody, it would have been a little while before Tony was killed. While the party was going on; after I left it and went up to the room because I had a headache. Is that what you mean, Mrs. Mason?"

"I don't know when," Gladys said. "But—yes, I suppose it would have been then."

"No," Lauren said. "I mean, it wasn't. I had this headache—the noise, the—the strain. Everything. I went up to the room, yes. I took aspirin and lay down. Then, after about half an hour, I took a Nembutal and I was—I was asleep when you came to tell me, wasn't I, Mrs. North?"

"Half asleep," Pam said.

"I remember everything I did at first," Lauren said. "Afterward—afterward it was hazy. I said that, when—when I came to ask you what I'd said, Mrs. North. But not at first. I took aspirin and lay down and then the Nembutal, when the aspirin didn't seem to

help. My nerves were jumping. And then I got that—
that soft feeling. You know what I mean? Anyway,
that's what I call it. The 'soft' feeling. And then
somebody knocked at the door and you came
in and—"

She stopped.

"I'm making this long," she said. "I know that. But,
I'm remembering it step by step. That's why. And—I
never once looked out the window. Came up, took my
dress off and my shoes. Went to the bathroom and
took the aspirin, and got a Nembutal capsule and a
glass of water and put them by the bed and—and got
on the bed and propped my head up and—and waited.
I didn't look out the window. Why should I? There—
there's nothing to see from the window. Oh, lots of
things. But not really anything. So—I didn't see anybody I knew—knew shouldn't be there, was out of
place—going into the King Arthur." She looked from
one to the other. "Don't you see?" she said, and
looked at Gladys Mason. "I was only dreaming. I
was—I must have been reciting a dream I was having.
I don't remember the dream at all, but that has to be
it."

She still spoke slowly. There was weight on each
word.

"Don't you understand?" Lauren said. "I'm sorry if
I worried you, Mrs. Mason. About—what did you say
his name was? Oh yes, Robert. Terribly sorry. I didn't
see him. I didn't see anybody."

Gladys Mason looked at Pam, and her eyes waited.
There was, Pam thought, uncertainty in Gladys's
eyes.

"Of course, dear," Faith Constable said. "Dreams
are such jumbles."

Which, Pam thought, was entirely true. Dreams are

178

made of shadows and of words; dreams start from something and go anywhere and nowhere. One sees the name of a hotel on a sign and, somewhere, perhaps at some other time, a man limping, and the dreaming mind makes a fantastic story embodying both. The dreams are sometimes pictures; sometimes words. (Jerry has told her that his are always in words, and that what wears him out is editing sentence structures.) It might well be such a dream which had brought them hurrying northeast through darkness to this bright house. No—not quite that. What had brought them still was real enough.

"Mrs. Payne," Pam said, "he hasn't been here? Robert Mason, I mean?"

"Why," Lauren said, "no. Not while I've been here. But that's only about an hour. You see—"

She had taken an early afternoon train to New Canaan, which is the nearest railway station to Ridgefield—the nearest, at any rate, with anything approaching adequate service. When she and Payne had gone into New York several days earlier, they had left their car in a New Canaan parking lot. When she had tried to start the car this afternoon it had refused to start. She thought that was about three o'clock. She had had to walk to a garage, wait for somebody to be free; afterward to wait, reading (for want of anything more fascinating) catalogues of new cars, while a mechanic found what had blocked the fuel line.

It had been after six when, finally, she got home. She had fixed herself a drink, a sandwich. Which reminded her. She really must get them—

"No," Pam said. She had a second thought. "Not yet, anyway," she said. "And nobody has come? Not the boy? Not anybody?"

"No. Why should anybody? Why should—" Again

she hesitated over the name. "Robert? I don't—" She stopped abruptly. She had been facing Pam; she turned quickly to Gladys Mason.

"You told him," she said. *"This—this thing you made out of what I said."* She breathed deeply, and spoke more slowly, but it seemed to Pam with an effort. "So now," she said, "he thinks I will tell somebody I saw him. Going into the other hotel. Carrying a rifle? That's what—that's why you came. You thought he might come here to—to make sure I didn't talk. That's it, isn't it?"

Mrs. Mason said, "Well—"

"Yes," Pam said. "That's it, of course."

"You've rather put me on the spot, haven't you?" Lauren said to Gladys Mason. "On quite a spot. And, you must be quite sure he did kill Tony, mustn't you? That if I *had* been looking out the window I could have seen him, because he was there. I didn't, but I could have. Because otherwise, what I might say wouldn't matter, would it?"

"I suppose—" Gladys began, and her voice was even duller than before, even more distant.

"No," Pam said. "Anyway, it's not as certain as you say. He might have come to tell you you were wrong. Or, to say, 'Look at me. I'm not the one you saw, am I?' It might be that."

"Fortunately," Faith Constable said, "it isn't either, is it, darlings? Because as far as we know, he hasn't come. Or, if he came before you got here, Lauren dear, he—he just found you weren't home and went away again."

"To return," Lauren said, with some bitterness. "A fine spot, a lovely spot." She shrugged delicate shoulders under the black dress. She turned to Pam. "You said 'anybody,' " she pointed out. "Is there somebody else who might come gunning for me?"

"We stopped at a drugstore in the village," Pam said. "To ask how to get here. The man at the counter said—just happened to say—that somebody had already asked. That two men had, actually. One early in the afternoon. A tall, young man. Who might have come up by bus. The other, just before we did—before I did. Another tall man. He had a car. Anyway, the soda clerk thought he had a car. He gave them both directions."

"Nobody," Lauren said. "Nobody's come."

"You're not expecting anybody?"

Pam thought Lauren hesitated a moment, looked involuntarily at the wide window which faced toward the drive. But when she answered, Lauren Payne said, "Why no. Nobody," and there was a note of surprise in her low voice. Then she said, "The man with a car. If he was ahead of you, he should be here by now, shouldn't he? Whoever he was? Of course, he could have got lost. Or changed his mind. Or stopped somewhere, perhaps for—" She smiled, her smile impartial for all. "You really must let me get you something," she said. "A drink, at least. You've come all the way up here like—like the cavalry to the rescue. And I—"

"Somebody," Faith Constable said, "is coming now."

They looked toward the window. Down the slope, beyond the hedge walls, the lights of a car were turning into the drive. The lights began to move up the drive. The lights seemed muted. Fog had formed while they talked.

14

Outwardly, there is little to distinguish Bill Weigand's Buick from any other Buick of its age and weight. There are, however, certain modifications, a longer radio antenna being the most obvious. There is also a switch which one may touch when it is desirable to have red headlights supplement white lights. If a certain button is touched, the Buick howls mournfully. And as the car went, far more rapidly than allowed, up the Saw Mill River Parkway a radio, set to police frequency, muttered to itself.

Sitting beside Bill, Jerry North leaned forward in his seat, as if he sought somehow to outspeed the car. Without words, he said, "Faster! Faster!"

"Will you for God's sake relax?" Bill said, when they were above Hawthorne Circle, and going seventy in a forty zone. "She'll be all right."

"Oh," Jerry said, "she'll be wonderful. If she's all right I'll wring her neck."

In spite of everything—of his own feeling of urgency, of his own worry—Bill Weigand laughed briefly at the idea of Jerry's laying harsh hands on any part of Pam's anatomy.

"It's all very fun—" Jerry began, and a siren behind drowned out his voice.

Bill slowed the Buick and let the parkway patrol come alongside. Then he touched his own siren and slowed further, letting the cruiser pull ahead. Then he turned on the red headlights. The cruiser tooted recognition. Bill went back to seventy.

"What it is," Jerry said, "she's gone to help somebody. That's what it always is, damn it."

Which was true enough.

"Well?" Jerry said.

It was anybody's guess. Probably to help Lauren Payne, whom Pam thought to be in danger. In danger, presumably, because she knew too much. Therefore, because she had heard too much or seen too much. A murderer with something the matter with his legs. But still they were guessing.

"There's a State Police barracks in Ridgefield," Bill said, and spoke patiently, since he had been saying much the same thing at quite frequent intervals since he had picked Jerry up at Jerry's office, and started to cover some sixty miles in as few minutes as possible. "They're keeping an eye on things."

He did not qualify this in words. His mind qualified. The State Police would have no reason to feel urgency. They would have other things to do. Cops can never be everywhere at once.

"Damn it all," Jerry said. "Why did she have to be so damned—cryptic? She doesn't have to be, you know. When she wants, she can be as—"

"I know," Bill said. "I suppose because she wanted a head start, don't you? Give us something to go on, but not too much. All right—why? She's yours, after all."

"How the hell would I—" Jerry said, more or less automatically, and stopped. "I suppose," he said, "a particularly lame dog, don't you? Or, one she thinks may be. She's always on your side, you know. Basically."

"Oh," Bill said, "of course. And often right."

"Only, she sticks her neck out."

"She sure as hell does," Bill said, and added, "Damn."

The last word saluted, angrily, the start of fog. Fog in the country is likely, is on windless nights almost inevitable, in late autumn, particularly where reservoirs abound. They were almost at the end of the parkway when there was the first puff of fog; they were through it with just time to notice it. But within minutes there was a patch—a patch, this time, not a puff. Bill checked speed slightly before they were through it, and the lights ahead showed clear again.

From the end of the Saw Mill on it was a most irritating fog—for seconds so dense that it could only be crept through and approaching cars, creeping too, were within feet before their headlights showed; then vanishing suddenly for several hundred yards, so that dipped headlights could be raised again and speed a little increased. Very exasperating, intolerably slow. There was nothing to do about it. They could only sit and hate it.

It was well after seven when, finally, they turned off Ridgefield's Main Street, went down and then up to the State Police barracks on a ridge.

"Nothing we've heard of," the desk sergeant said. "All tucked in for the night, she seemed to be, last time we looked. Listen, Captain, you don't think she—"

"No," Bill said. "That is, I've no reason to think so. You've kept an eye on the place?"

"Well," the sergeant said, and hesitated. "Well—turned out we couldn't. Not the way we planned. Had to pull the man off. Helluva smashup over on Seven. Foggy as hèll down there—it's in a valley most of the time—and some bastard tried to pass at sixty and—well, we had to cover. But—"

"Tell me how to get to the house," Bill said. "And—somebody'd better come along. You've got somebody?"

"Well—wait a minute." He got up from the desk and went into a rear room. He came back with a lieutenant. "We're short," the lieutenant said. "We're always short. You really need somebody?"

"I'm out of jurisdiction," Bill said. "Right—I hope I'll need somebody who isn't."

"Trail along, Jonesy," the lieutenant said. "Or—you want him to show the way?"

"Sergeant Jones had better show the way," Bill said.

The lights came up the drive slowly; there was a kind of uncertainty in the movement, as if the car groped its way. The fog isn't that heavy, Pam thought, and in the same instant knew the thought was absurd. Even a light night fog—a veil of fog—is a blanket from within a moving car; a soft white blanket which throws treacherous light back into baffled eyes.

"Who ever can *this* be?" Lauren asked—asked anybody—and got up from her chair by the fire and walked down the room toward the door. She looked frail walking away from them, very slender indeed in the close-fitting black dress. "The poor darling," Faith Constable said. "However she felt about Tony—" She left that unfinished.

The car came so slowly that it was still a little way down the drive, and beyond the hemlock hedge, when Lauren opened the door, and at the same time turned on the terrace light. She stepped out onto the terrace and stepped from the sight of those—of Pam and Faith and Gladys Mason—who still sat by the fire. The car groped its way into the turnaround and car lights went off. The car moved on for a few more feet and then it, too, was out of sight.

It was Pam who moved, to one side and toward the window, so that through it the car would again be in sight. But she had only started to move when there was the sharp, deadly crack of a rifle. In the same instant there was a scream, cut off.

Pam ran toward the door and was conscious, although she did not look back, that one of the others ran after her. It took her only seconds to reach the open door.

Lauren lay a little way outside the door, crumpled on the flags.

One door of the car was open. Beside the car, just beyond the full reach of the terrace light, two dark figures were locked together, and swayed together.

They were, Pam thought, struggling for something held between them.

She knelt beside Lauren, who moaned, and Pam said, "Lauren. *Mrs Payne!*" Only the low, wordless sound of moaning answered her.

Somebody was on the other side of Lauren, bent down over her. Gladys Mason.

"Help me carry her," Gladys said, and squatted, put her arms gently under the slender woman. "On your side," she said, and Pam put her hands under Lauren's body. "Now," Gladys said, and they lifted, and Pam thought, she's doing almost all of it. But should we have left her there until—?

Faith was standing in the door, looking at them, looking beyond them to the car.

There was sound from there now—the sound of feet scuffling on gravel. Pam did not look back, nor did Gladys. Between them, slowly, carefully, they carried Lauren into the room, down it a little way to a wide sofa. She kept on moaning.

Gladys bent over her.

"The shoulder, I think," she said. "She's bleeding a good deal. We'll have to try to stop it." Then she said, "Mrs. Payne? Can you hear me?"

She was not answered.

It was still slow going, but the police car they followed knew its way, and Weigand tail-gated. After a little less than a mile, the right-hand direction light on the police car began to blink. Bill slowed and followed onto a narrower, blacktop road. It was just as he finished the turn that he and Jerry heard, ahead of them, seemingly a little to the left, the sharp crack of a shot.

"God!" Jerry said. "Hurry."

"It could be a hunter," Weigand said. "Somebody out after—"

"Damn it, hurry!"

It was as if the car ahead heard him. The car jumped away from them; Bill's Buick jumped after it, and Bill hoped—hoped anxiously—that Jones knew the road as well as he seemed to think he knew it, and that they would have the road to themselves.

It was a short ride, too fast in fog. They were on the right shoulder once; again they were much too far to the left. But then the tail signal of the police car blinked again, this time on the left, and the car slowed abruptly, and began to turn.

For an instant, Jerry, on the right, saw—was almost

certain he saw—the outlines of a car parked on the shoulder of the narrow road, a few yards beyond the turning point. Then, as Bill turned behind the police car up the drive, the parked shadow vanished.

Jerry clutched for something, anything, as the Buick checked. He caught himself against the dashboard padding.

The police car had stopped, at the same time pulling sharply to the right.

In its lights, and now in theirs, they could see a tall man running down the drive toward them. He seemed to run uncertainly and, after the lights caught him, to be running only because he had run before, now could not quickly stop himself. Then he began to run to the left, toward lawn and bushes; obviously toward concealment.

Bill wrenched at the door on his side and it began to open. But then Bill stopped its opening.

Sergeant Jones was already out of the police car; was running toward the tall uncertain man and, as he ran, tugging at the gun on his hip.

"I hope to God he doesn't—" Bill said, but by then the man who had been running toward them stopped running, turned back onto the drive, walked slowly. After a moment, he put his hands up. He said, "Don't shoot," and his voice sounded very young, sounded frightened.

Jonesy took hold of him. He seemed to be shaking him.

There was room to pull up alongside the police car, and Bill moved the Buick there. The lights of both cars were on the State Police sergeant and the tall, thin man he held.

"I didn't do anything," the held man said. "I—it wasn't me. I just—"

"Hold it," Jones said, his voice hard, rough. He

turned and looked toward the other car. "Says he didn't do anything," Jones said, his harsh voice derisive.

Bill guessed.

"You're Mason?" he said. "Robert Mason?"

"I didn't do anything," the tall man—the tall youth—said, and his voice shook. "Suppose I'm Robert Mason? I didn't—"

"Bring him along," Bill said, and the Buick leaped at the slope of the drive, spitting gravel behind it. At the far end of the drive the house was long, glowed with light.

A man was on hands and knees on the gravel of the turnaround, near one of two cars standing in it. He seemed to be trying to get up. He shook his head from side to side.

As Bill and Jerry North reached him, bent to help him up, they saw that there was a gash on the side of his head. As they lifted him, blood splattered from the wound.

When they had got him to his feet, he slumped between them. They turned him so that light fell on his face.

"Self," Bill said. "What the hell's he—"

He did not finish.

They had to carry James Self across the terrace, through the open door.

A man was kneeling beside someone stretched on a sofa; he was rubbing a hand he held; he was saying, "Lauren. Lauren!" But then, as he heard them enter, he turned, and almost instantly was on his feet and began to come toward them.

"The murdering bastard!" he said. "I'll kill the—"

Jerry suddenly found that he was supporting the entire weight of James Self. He began to move Self toward the nearest chair.

Bill went to meet the advancing man.

"Take it easy, Smythe," Bill said. "Somebody's done enough for now."

Blaine Smythe stopped. He said, "Where the hell've you been? He's killed—"

He threw his hands out, hopelessly. He turned back toward the sofa.

But now there was a woman kneeling there, tearing sheets, making a pad of sheets, pressing the pad down on the body of Lauren Payne. Lauren's face was startlingly white; lipstick on her lips was a kind of mockery. A black dress had been torn down from the left side of her body, and it was there the sheet pad was being pressed.

Jerry put Self down in a chair, and Self slumped in it. But then he opened his eyes and looked at Jerry and said, in a mumble, "Pushed it at me. Tried to make me—" Then he closed his eyes again, and appeared, once more, to lose consciousness.

Jerry turned away from the chair. As he turned his foot hit something, and what it hit skittered a few feet on tile flooring. What he had kicked, and kicked from a chair's shadow into light, was a rifle.

"Tell her to hurry," the kneeling woman said to— people were beginning to become identifiable—Faith Constable. "There's still a good deal of blood."

"She's hurrying as fast as she can," Faith said, and then, from some distance, Jerry heard Pam say, "It's an emergency, operator. I don't know any numbers. A doctor—an ambulance—listen—I'm at the Payne house—on Nod Road—how do I know? Wilton. Ridgefield. How do I know? Listen—*a woman's dying*. Do you hear me? We've got to have help. I—"

Jerry saw her, then. She was at the far end of the long room, in a corner of it. She was standing by a table and her voice was high. There was anger in her voice. "If you'll only listen," Pam said, and there was desperation in her voice.

Jerry started down the room toward her.

Then a car door slammed outside and Jones's harsh voice scraped into the room. "Get along in there, you," Jones said. Then Robert Mason was propelled into the room, Sergeant Jones behind him.

Jerry was nearest. Bill had gone to the sofa, was bending down over Lauren, saying something to the woman who still tried to stop the flow of blood from Lauren's slender body. Bill was saying something to the woman, who looked up at him, shook her head.

"Sergeant," Jerry said, and moved toward Jones. "I'll take this one. Get on the telephone in your car. We need an ambulance—a doctor." He pointed toward Lauren, the others by the sofa.

Jones shoved the tall youth into Jerry North's hands. Jones ran across the terrace and the drive to the police car.

Bill had replaced the sturdy woman who had been giving what first aid she could. He was leaning close to Lauren, had lifted the sheet padding. He stood up, and the woman replaced him.

"It seems to be in the shoulder," Bill said. "At a guess, nothing vital hit. If we can stop the—"

"She's dying," Blaine Smythe said, and spoke loudly—almost shouted the words. "The bastard's killed her. The way he killed Tony." He was standing, on the far side of the sofa. At first, he did not seem to speak directly to anyone. But then he turned to Bill Weigand. "For God's sake," Blaine Smythe said. *"I saw him, Captain!* This time I saw him."

Bill looked at Blaine Smythe for a moment, and then shook his head.

"No," he said, "I don't think Mrs. Payne is dying, Mr. Smythe. I'm not even sure she's badly hurt.

Shock. And some loss of blood. I think Mrs. Mason's checked that—Mrs. Mason and the others, of course."

"You're not a doctor," Smythe said, his voice bitter.

"Right," Bill Weigand said, "I'm not a doctor. Some experience with gunshot wounds but, as you say, not a doctor. A policeman, Mr. Smythe. I'll—"

He stopped and looked toward the door, as Sergeant Jones came through it.

"On their way," he said, and looked around the room. "What the hell," Sergeant Jones said, "goes on here?"

15

We look, Pamela North thought, like the cast—the rather large cast—of a play, assembled for a climactic scene. It ought to be a comedy; this large and uncluttered, this glass-walled room—this almost drawing room—is the setting for comedy. We should all be quick and witty, in an early Noel Cowardish fashion, and when the curtain comes down it should come down on a quip. Only, some of us are a little bunged up for comedy. She looked around the room, counting. Ten including Jerry and me, but we're really in the audience. This isn't Bill's way at all, Pam thought, but I don't see how, this time, he can get out of it.

Ten, including them. Lauren Payne, propped by pillows on a sofa; pale still, but not so strangely pale; wearing a house robe of a coppery tone a little deeper than her shining hair. And Blaine Smythe, sitting in a chair by the sofa, looking anxiously at Lauren, giving the impression of hovering over her.

Blaine had been the one who, most emphatically,

most anxiously, had protested Lauren's decision. It had been a simple decision, simply phrased. "I want to stay. I'm going to stay." After a time the doctor had merely shrugged; had said, "All right, Mrs. Payne. I can't make you be sensible."

But the doctor, who had arrived surprisingly soon after Sergeant Jones had telephoned for help, had seemed more annoyed than concerned. He had examined Lauren's shoulder and said, "Nice clean wound, anyway," and lifted her gently and looked at the back of her shoulder and said, "Ummm, didn't come out too bad. Move your arm a little, Mrs. Payne. Hurt too much? So." He had examined further. "You'll be all right," he said. "Better take you in to Norwalk, though. Just to be on the safe side."

"No," Lauren said then, "I want to stay. Until— I'm going to stay."

The doctor would not advise it, but—skip Norwalk hospital. At least until morning. He'd know more in the morning. He bandaged as he talked. Rest—go to bed. He'd give her something to help her sleep. If there was somebody who could stay with her? "You," he said, and looked at Gladys Mason. "You seem competent enough. At least, you don't seem to have done all the wrong things, and lost your head. Eh?"

"Of course," Gladys Mason said. Her voice was dull again, not quick as it had been when she had, rather unexpectedly, taken charge.

"No," Lauren said. Her low voice had gained some strength. "Not until—until it's settled. If you'll help—"

Gladys had helped—had supported her out of the room and, after a time, back into the room, now wearing the coppery housecoat.

Blaine had used the time of their absence to protest—to the physician, to Weigand, to Faith Constable. Lauren couldn't be allowed to do this. She was worse hurt than she thought. It was criminal to let her do this, brutal to let her do this. He had, finally, succeeded in annoying the physician.

"You talk too much," the physician said, and there was a growl in his voice. "If she had to go to the hospital, I'd take her to the hospital. If she had to go to bed and have a nurse, I'd see she went to bed and had a nurse. Actually, it's a superficial wound. A good deal of bleeding, but people can spare a bit of blood."

"She was unconscious," Blaine Smythe said. "You talk as if it was only a scratch."

"Shock," the doctor said. "Some get it and some don't. You're going to have a black eye in a few hours. You know that? Now, let's look at this one."

"This one" was James Self, who was conscious by then and had started to get up out of the chair and subsided back into it. Since then he had merely sat, his eyes half closed, his body slumped. When the doctor started to examine the gash on the side of his head, Self said, "Leave it alone, for God's sake." The doctor had not left it alone.

Certainly too much bunging up for drawing-room comedy, Pam thought. And, a uniformed State Police sergeant sitting in a straight chair near the door, with a rifle across his knees. Not a comedy character at all. She shivered slightly. Poor Robert Mason, silent, in a cheap suit which gaped from the back of his neck, slumped forward in his chair, hands—hands somehow too large for the rest of him—dangling between his knees. The poor, lost boy. But—safe boy now. Everybody safe but a man named James Self; the rather abrupt, not too pleasant, man named Self. So, now it was really simple. All over but the arresting.

Only, why then didn't Bill merely arrest Self, or have the trooper arrest him, and let them all go home?

A silly damn fool way to go about it, Bill Weigand thought, half sitting on a long table, facing all of them. Theatrical and, heaven knew, cluttered. And the sort of situation in which, almost inevitably, everybody starts talking at once, once anybody starts at all. So far, nobody had, except James Self. James Self's remark had been brief, and final, and uttered a little groggily.

"You're a goddamn liar," Self had said, to Blaine Smythe, after Smythe had said, "I saw him, Captain. This time I saw him."

Everybody had waited for Self to continue. Self had not continued.

Start somewhere, Bill told himself, and lighted a cigarette. Find out, as Sergeant Jones had suggested, what the hell went on here—what had caused this assemblage, which amounted almost to a convention, in the middle of nowhere; what had so muddled what he had begun to think an essentially simple thing, to be disclosed by a couple of reasonably simple questions.

"So," Bill Weigand said, "I take it, Mr. Self, you deny shooting Mrs. Payne? And, of course, her husband?"

"You can take it," Self said. "I've nothing against Mrs. Payne. Never had. Just a woman out of luck." He paused and looked across some feet at Lauren Payne, who had closed her eyes. "Far's I know, anyway," Self said. "As for Payne, he was an all-American rat. I'm not, however, a rat-catcher." He fingered the bandage on his head. "He's got living teammates, apparently," Self added, and looked at Blaine Smythe. Smythe continued to look, anxiously, at Lauren Payne. He did not look at Self.

196

"Right," Bill said. "You didn't shoot Mrs. Payne. Didn't kill Mr. Payne. What brought you here?"

"Ask Mrs. Payne," Self said.

Bill turned toward Lauren Payne, and she opened her eyes.

"I don't know," she said. "I don't know what he means."

Her deep voice was very low; it was clear, but it seemed that she spoke with an effort. Which was, certainly, reasonable enough.

Self looked at her steadily for some seconds. Then he started to get up from the chair, pushing with his hands on the arms. Suddenly, he gave it up and slumped back again into the chair.

"Have it your own way," he said, and his voice was weary as the woman's. "For now."

Then he, too, closed his eyes. Bill started toward him, and Self opened his eyes. "I'm all right," he said. "Bloody but unbowed. Let them get it out of their systems, why don't you?" He closed his eyes again.

"Right," Bill said. "Mr. Smythe, you want to get it out of your system? You saw Mr. Self fire the shot? At Mrs. Payne?"

"You're damn right. Stopped the car, opened the door part way, fired from inside. Then got out, holding the gun." He turned toward Weigand, gestured toward the door. "The one the sergeant's got," he said.

"Right," Bill said. "Where were you?"

"Running at him. He was getting ready to fire again. I was too late the first time but the second—I grabbed him. If I hadn't—she was just lying there—the second time—"

He reached out toward the slight woman whose eyes were closed in a white face. He touched her hand, but then withdrew his own. Then he said, "Are you all right, Lauren?"

197

She nodded her head without opening her eyes.

"Where did you run from, Mr. Smythe?" Bill asked him, and for a second, as he turned back toward Weigand, Smythe seemed puzzled.

"Oh," he said, "I see what you mean. I was behind the hedge."

"Why?"

"Well—" Smythe said, and hesitated. "All right, I was afraid something like this might happen. I wanted to stop its happening." He paused again. "All right," he said. "The date I told you I had. It was here. With—with whoever came to hurt Lauren."

"You thought Mr. Self was planning to hurt Mrs. Payne? Why?"

Then Blaine Smythe looked away from Weigand and toward Gladys Mason and her son, who sat side by side. Gladys had a hand on her son's arm. The gangling boy did not seem aware of this. Smythe looked at them for a moment, and then back at Weigand.

"No," he said, "not Self. I was wrong. It's one reason I was—slow. I—I didn't expect a car, you see. Didn't think the kid had a car. Thought—all right, I was a damn fool. A blundering damn fool. Lauren might have been—for all I did to stop it, he might have killed her."

He spoke bitterly. He looked again at Lauren, as if, Pam thought, he sought understanding. Lauren did not open her eyes. The poor thing, Pam thought, this *is* too much for her. She's—she's all drained. The doctor ought to have made her—

"You mean you were expecting Mr. Mason," Bill said. "Why? What would he have against Mrs. Payne?"

Again Blaine Smythe hesitated, again looked at Lauren Payne, and again she seemed not to notice.

"All right," he said. "I've got to tell them, Lauren.

She—she was looking out the window. In her hotel room. She saw somebody going into the hotel across the street. Somebody—limping. She wasn't sure but—it looked like the kid. He limps, you know."

"No," Weigand said. "I didn't know that. Do you, Mr. Mason?" The boy did not move. "Mr. Mason?"

"Sometimes," Robert Mason said. "When I'm tired."

"You knew Mrs. Payne had seen somebody she thought might be you?"

"I don't know what she thought. I wasn't there, so she couldn't have seen me. But, what she said to Mother—" He stopped, looked at his mother.

"I told him," she said. "I was wrong to tell him. But—"

"What did you tell him?"

Slowly, as if each word were heavier than the one before, Mrs. Mason repeated what she had told her son.

"Something the matter with his legs," Weigand repeated, and looked at Pam North. He said, "Oh."

"Well," Pam said, "we wanted to see that Bobby—"

Weigand continued to look at her.

"All right," she said, "only he didn't, did he? So—" He continued to look. "All right," she said. "I'm sorry, Bill. I grovel. We all grovel."

"Mrs. Payne," Weigand said, "you did see somebody? Somebody with something the matter with his legs? Somebody you thought might have been going into the King Arthur, to a place from which he could shoot your husband?"

"I don't remember what I said," Lauren said. "I don't remember saying anything."

"Or—seeing anything. This man. I suppose it was a man?"

"I don't remember," she said. "Oh—perhaps I did. Perhaps—perhaps it will come back to me. I'd taken something, you see, and it's all—foggy. But perhaps—" She sighed, leaned back.

Bill asked her if she was sure she was up to this; sure she shouldn't be away from it, in bed. She said, "Not yet, Captain. Not until it's—" And did not finish the sentence. Bill waited a moment. She moved her head from side to side, as if even so slight a movement exhausted her.

"This is too much for her," Smythe said, and spoke sharply. "You can't go on with this."

"She'll have to decide," Bill said. "She apparently has. Mr. Mason—"

Robert Mason did not look up. He gazed at the floor, between his dangling hands.

"Bobby!" his mother said, and he looked at her. "Answer him, dear," Gladys Mason said. He looked at her. "Answer him." He looked at Bill Weigand.

"What brought you here?" Bill said. "And, why did you run?"

"She said she saw me," the thin-faced boy said. He looked at Bill Weigand, his eyes dark. "I wanted her to look at me so she'd know she'd made a mistake." He paused. "I keep thinking," he said, almost as if he spoke to himself, "I keep thinking maybe I'll get a break."

"You didn't see her?"

"Not until now. Until you and the cop dragged me in. You want me to ask her now? All right. Mrs. Payne, did you see me across the street? Carrying a gun, maybe? Only, I haven't got a gun. Not any more, I haven't. And I wasn't—Mrs. Payne, why don't you listen to me? Look at me?"

Lauren leaned against the back of the sofa. She did not open her eyes. "Leave her alone, damn you!"

Blaine Smythe said. "She's said she doesn't remember."

Robert Mason continued to look at Lauren. But she did not look at him, and he turned back to Weigand.

"She wasn't here earlier," he said. "I came up—"

He had, he said, come up to Ridgefield by bus. He had sought and got directions to the Payne house, and had walked to it—walked the three miles to it—and found no one there. He had waited around for a while—maybe an hour, maybe longer. He hadn't noticed. He had got hungry; had walked back to the village; found a bakery-delicatessen and got a sandwich and a cup of coffee. He had thought he might as well give it up, go back to New York. But he had found there was no bus for a long time and decided he might as well go back to the house.

"I was coming up the drive," he said, "and I heard this shot. So—I didn't want to be around if there was another shooting. Another shooting somebody might try to pin on me. So—all right, I ran."

"Before you ran, you didn't see anything?" Bill asked him.

The boy hesitated. You could almost see his mind work, Pam thought—see a frightened mind scurrying.

"Somebody jumped up from behind—well, I know now it's the hedge. Then, it was just a shadow—a shadow of someone running—against a—a sort of dark wall."

"After you heard the shot."

"Sure. I thought—well, I thought whoever had been hiding behind the hedge was the man who had fired the shot. And there I was maybe—oh, fifty feet away—and I couldn't prove I hadn't—and she'd said—maybe she'd said—she saw me going into the other hotel so—so I ran."

He had gained some animation as he spoke. It left him suddenly. He said, dully, "That's all," and began, again, to stare down at the floor.

"Mrs. Payne," Bill Weigand said and she, like the boy, seemed not at first to hear him. He repeated her name, and she opened her eyes and looked at him.

"You still don't remember?" Bill said. "You've seen Mr. Mason now. Was it he you saw? Has it, as you say, come back to you?"

She looked at him for some seconds.

"No," she said, "it hasn't come back to me, Captain. I'm still—confused about it. It's still—a kind of blur."

But this time her voice was steady; her voice did not in the least reflect confusion. Why, Pam North thought, it isn't the way she says. It's—she's saying something else. Something else entirely. And—she's waiting for something.

"Mrs. Payne," Bill said, "I've got to ask you this— you didn't—make up this story? About a man limping? Perhaps, about seeing a man at all?"

She did not seem in the least surprised by the question.

"No," she said. "I didn't make anything up. But—I may have dreamed something, mayn't I?" She looked, then, at Blaine Smythe, sitting so near her, with so anxious a face. "You understand what I mean, don't you, Blaine?" she said. He said, "Of course, dear," and turned again toward Bill Weigand, his face angry. "Can't you leave her alone?"

"No," Bill said. "Not anybody. You're quite certain you saw Mr. Self fire a rifle? Not merely start to get out of a car, perhaps holding something?"

"Holding a rifle," Blaine said. "Firing a rifle. What do you mean, something? You've got the gun, haven't you?"

"Yes," Bill said. "You saw him fire. Ran across and grabbed him. I gather you struggled for the gun. That you hit him with it. That at some time during the tussle, he hit you. You are getting a black eye, you know."

"I hit him," Smythe said. "Or he banged into it. Hell, we weren't fighting for points. It was—it was a scramble. First to keep him from shooting Lauren again. Then—well, I figured he'd just as soon shoot me."

"Right," Bill said. "Natural you should." He turned toward James Self, who had not moved from the deep chair and now did not move in it. But it was entirely clear from his eyes that he wasn't groggy anymore. His eyes were very watchful, now. "Well, Mr. Self," Bill said, "you still say you didn't—"

The telephone at the end of the room rang. Its ringing was a loud violence in the room. For a moment, nobody moved to answer the telephone. Then Gladys Mason started to stand up, but Pam said, "No, I'll get it. Probably it's that operator to say that this is Wilton. Or Ridgefield. Or—" She did not finish, walked toward the telephone, said, "Hello?" into it. Then she said, "Hello, Sergeant. Yes, he is." She put the receiver down on the table and started to walk back, and said, "Bill, it's—" But by then Bill Weigand was moving, quickly, down the room toward her, and toward the telephone.

There was complete silence in the room as Bill spoke on the telephone. He said, "O.K., Sergeant. Go ahead." Then he listened. Then he said, "Who could ask for anything more?" and they heard the click of the receiver going back in the cradle. It was, Pam thought, an extremely disappointing conversation. Bill came back. He said, "Well, Mr. Self? What do you say happened? If not what Mr. Smythe says did? Or—"

"Nope," Self said. "I still didn't. Either one." He seemed to consider. Then he said, "Mrs. Payne, do you say you didn't call me up this afternoon? Tell me what was evidently a cock and bull story?"

She did not speak immediately, but looked down the room at him. Then she said, "No, Mr. Self. I didn't call you."

"And," Self said, "I've called Tony Payne a rat and you, Captain, have got it fixed in your mind why, haven't you?"

"Go ahead," Bill said.

"And Mrs. Payne maybe did and maybe didn't see somebody, but if she did whoever she saw might want to keep her quiet. Only, I don't limp, you know. Unless you want to say I faked a limp. As some sort of disguise?"

"Mr. Self, why don't you just tell us—"

"Patience," Self said. "And, of course, fortitude." Suddenly he smiled as if amused. "And maybe what they call in the theater voluntary suspension of disbelief. Isn't that what they call it, Smythe? You lying son of a—" He did not finish. Blaine Smythe might not have heard.

"All right," Self said. "Mrs. Payne—make it somebody who said she was Mrs. Payne—called me up this afternoon. At the shop. She said—"

She had said she wanted him to come up to the house. She had given him reason enough to come.

Bill Weigand shook his head then. He said that that was not good enough. Self raised his eyebrows. "No," Bill said.

James Self seemed to consult inwardly. He reached a decision. He said, "O.K. What she said was—"

The woman who had identified herself as Lauren Payne had asked him to come up and get a girl named Jo-An Rhodes. The woman who said she was Lauren

Payne said that she had come home and found Miss Rhodes in her house, going through "my husband's papers." Surprised, Jo-An had become almost hysterical; was still hysterical at the moment of the call. She kept saying, "I wrote him letters. Somebody will show Jim the letters."

"She said," Self said, his voice level, without expression, "that she knew about Jo-An and her husband. And—that Jo-An worked for me. And that she—Mrs. Payne—didn't want to call the police, because she knew Jo-An didn't really plan to steal anything, but that technically, she supposed, it would be burglary and—well, a lot of stuff. And would I come and get Jo-An? So I got the car."

"And," Bill said, "didn't leave a message for Miss Rhodes?"

Self looked at him and shook his head.

"She came to me," Bill said. "Said you were missing. That it wasn't like you to go without leaving word at the shop."

Self said, "Oh." Then he said, "I wouldn't have if I thought she was up here, would I?" He looked at Bill Weigand, who nodded his head.

So—Self had, he said, got his car and driven to Ridgefield. He had stopped in the village at a drugstore for directions. At that, Pam felt a little like raising her hand.

"You drove directly here?"

Pam took down her mental hand. And James Self shook his head.

"Got lost," he said. "I damn near always do. The kid, Jo-An, says— Anyway, I got lost. There's this Nod Road and then, farther along, there's a Nod Hill Road, for God's sake. The point being, obviously, to trap the unwary. So—"

So, missing Nod Road, he had driven on several

miles to Nod Hill Road, and on it for several more miles before he realized he had gone much too far, and found a house, and asked again—asked, this time, where the hell he was. He had been told; he had finally got to the Payne house.

"I started to get out of the car," Self said, "and this lying bastard—" He looked at Smythe. Smythe was looking at him, now; looking at Self with a smile which might have been of pity, and shaking his head slowly, in a kind of baffled disparagement. "This son of a bitch," Self said, "came rushing at me with something in his hands. I thought it was some kind of a club. Anyway, he tried to hit me with it, and I tried to take it away from him—by then I could feel what it was; it was this bloody gun—and we writhed around like a couple of extras in a Western film, and I got in a poke and then—well, then he slammed me. Next thing I knew, somebody was picking me up."

He stopped.

"A bald and unconvincing narrative," he said. "To which I can add no verisimilitude by corroborative detail. Mrs. Payne didn't call me. Jo-An obviously isn't here. This—" he paused—"animal, says I had the gun and shot Mrs. Payne with it. And, my fingerprints will be all over the gun, won't they? And, if I know this rat, and I'm beginning to, in all the right places, won't they? Because after he knocked me out, he could put them where he liked, couldn't he?"

"You heard the shot? If you didn't fire it?"

"Sure," Self said. "Only, I didn't realize what it was until I knew we were fighting over a gun. I had the windows of the car closed and it was before I opened the door and—well, it sounded a long way off. Anyway, you hear the damnedest things in the country." He looked at Weigand. "And I suppose that sounds thin, too," he said.

"You saw Mrs. Payne? Saw her fall after she was shot?"

"Movement," Self said. "A vague feeling there was somebody on the terrace. I was pulling up behind this other car. There was fog all over the windshield." He spread his hands. "I don't make it any better," he said. "It's true, but I don't make it any better. It—well, it all happened so damned fast."

"My God," Smythe said, in a tone of astonishment and of contempt. "Of all the—" He shook his head, apparently being unable to think of a word for such an enormity. "I hide behind a hedge and shoot a girl I came to take care of, and just at that moment—just at that moment, by God, Self drives up and I try to make him take the gun—my God, Captain!"

"It would be quite a coincidence," Bill said. "By the way, Mr. Smythe, how'd you get here?"

"Get here?"

Bill waited.

"Oh, see what you mean. I parked my car down on the road, and walked up. The idea—well, the idea was to catch anybody who might try to hurt Lauren. Not scare him away."

"You seemed pretty sure there would be someone. Why?"

"I was right, wasn't I? I don't know—don't you ever have hunches, Captain? Just—feelings? Anyway, after Lauren called me—" He stopped; looked at Lauren Payne.

"I telephoned him," Lauren said. "At the theater. I—I asked him to come up. I—I was afraid to be here alone. I thought—oh, I got to imagining things. When the car came up—Mr. Self's car—I thought it was Blaine. That's why I went out."

It's not coming together, Pam thought. It's coming apart. She said she wasn't expecting anyone—Pam interrupted herself, called herself a ninny. Lauren would hardly tell three other women that she had invited a man to a lonely house, in which she was alone, the night after her husband's murder. She, Pam, thought, hoped we would go away before he came.

"After Lauren called me," Blaine Smythe said, "I—well, I got to worrying. I thought, maybe she knows something. Maybe— And I knew about young Mason here. Tony had told me. Said the kid was nuts. That there was no telling what he'd— Anyway, I checked at the hotel—I know them there—and found the kid hadn't showed up for work and—" he spread his hands. Said that there they had it. And added that he was damn glad he had come, even if it wasn't the kid.

Bill Weigand merely listened. It seemed to Pam that he was merely waiting for Smythe to finish, waiting politely. Well, Self's story was as thin as he said it was—said it was before anyone else could, as clever liars do. Now Bill would say to the Connecticut policeman that he thought they had what they needed, and that he'd better take Mr. Self along for the time being and—

"Mrs. Constable," Weigand said, "you left the rehearsal of *Uprising* this afternoon after you had got a telephone call. Who called you?"

"Why," Faith said. "Gladys." One sensitive, expressive hand flickered toward the woman in dull black. "She wanted me to help her. Wanted somebody she could—somebody who could advise her. Why?"

"And you, or she, called Mrs. North, and she joined you and then—then you came up here? To see Mrs. Payne? Perhaps to warn her? And, hoping you could—intercept Robert before he had a chance to do harm? If he meant to do harm?'

"Yes. To do what we could."

"Mr. Simon didn't object to your leaving the rehearsal?"

"Lars?" There was surprise in her modulated voice. "Dear Lars?" Lars Simon, her voice said, would not do anything so preposterous. There was, Bill thought, the further suggestion that Lars had better not try. "Why do you ask that?"

"Oh," Bill said, "curiosity. Do you mind telling me something about the play, Mrs. Constable? When I went into the theater, Mr. Smythe here was sitting at a table, near the center of the stage. Mr. Simon—he was filling in for you, he told me afterward—came on and said—well, a sentence apparently ending, 'it was you who began it.' "

"Cues Blaine," Mrs. Constable said. "Second scene, second act. Yes?"

"You mind telling me something about the situation?"

She said, "Good heavens, man!" She looked around at the others; she shrugged her shoulders, deftly. Her hands flickered for a moment, registering incredulity and surprise.

"Please," Weigand said. "It may have bearing, Mrs. Constable."

"I don't," she said, "have any idea how much you want, Captain. Not the whole play?" He shook his head. "I thought not," she said. "And thank heaven not. Well—at that moment. There's a native uprising, you know. White settlers in peril. All that. They attack—the natives, that darling Tommy so fearsome with his sharp teeth—at the end of the first scene. Curtain. The second scene, it's the next morning. I come in and tell Blaine—who's George Silcox in the play—that he began it. Then—"

"Right," Bill said. "He's sitting on a chair by a

table. He has his right leg up on another chair. Why?"

"Why? Oh, the leg. Because he was shot in it, of course."

"Yes," Bill said. "I guessed it was something like that. This afternoon. Lars Simon didn't like the way Mr. Smythe moved when you—that is, when he—cued him. He said something like—" Bill paused, remembering words. "Like 'you've got to start wearing it. Otherwise you'll be skipping all over the place.' Wearing what, Mrs. Constable?"

But he did not wait for her answer. He turned, abruptly, toward Blaine Smythe, who now sat facing him, leaning a little forward in his chair.

"Perhaps I'd better ask you," Weigand said. "Wearing what, Mr. Smythe?"

Smythe looked at him for a moment, and then smiled; seemed to chuckle. He said, "Man, are you thorough! The bandage, of course. It's a—" He hesitated. "A sort of snap-on," he said. "The prop man ran it up. There's only a few minutes between the scenes. Just time for me to snap the gadget on my foot. Looks like a lot of bandaging from out front."

"That's all?"

"Sure—hell, you want me to draw a picture of it? Oh, the bandaging goes a good way up my leg. I'm wearing shorts, of course. Rough sort of splints—the old doc's had to make do with what he could, you see. And—well, there you are."

"You haven't been wearing it, I gather? During rehearsals?"

"Not when I can get out of it," Blaine said. "It's damn uncomfortable. Hot as hell and—"

Then he stopped, and the smile faded.

"What are you getting at?" he asked Bill Weigand.

"A man who limped," Bill said. "Used crutches, I think. Mrs. Payne?"

Lauren was no longer leaning back on the sofa. She was sitting straight, she was looking at Blaine Smythe, watching him. She turned, slowly, toward Bill Weigand.

"You didn't see who shot at you this evening? Or—did you? And, was it Mr. Self?"

She seemed surprised at the question; there was a vagueness on her face, an instant before intent.

"Why," she said, "no—not really. The fog—the terrace light seemed to bounce back from the fog. I saw the car and then—then something hit me. Like a hand hitting me, almost. I started to fall and heard a—a cracking sound. No, I didn't see who—tried to kill me."

"No," Bill said. "Do you want to tell me now, Mrs. Payne?"

She seemed, Pam thought, to know precisely what Bill meant. But she hesitated. She said, "Not yet."

"Mr. Smythe," Bill said, "I asked one of our men—Sergeant Mullins—to find this trick bandage. Took him a bit of time—Simon was out somewhere. But he ran it down. At the theater."

"I could have saved you—" Smythe began, but did not finish.

"Probably," Bill said. "Or—but never mind. A rifle is a rather awkward thing to carry around, of course. Even a light rifle. A long suitcase of some kind. But, we'd be looking for something like that, of course. Have been. On the other hand—you can put a rifle down inside a trouser leg. Strap it to the leg. But, the leg's stiff then, isn't it Mr. Smythe. However—if you have a bandage you can, as you say, snap on—and snap off, of course—the stiffness is explained, isn't it? Bandaged foot shows. Poor man's been in an automobile accident. Or broken his leg skiing. And—"

Smythe laughed. "You," he said, "ought to be writing plays. You're better than Lars."

"No," Bill said. "I didn't think of it, Mr. Smythe. And Lars Simon didn't. You did, didn't you?"

Smythe looked confident still. He said, "You're nuts, Captain. That's your trouble. You're—"

"No," Bill said. "I told you we got hold of this trick bandage of yours. There's a streak down it, Mr. Smythe. Narrow, but very straight. Straight as the barrel of a rifle. Streak made by oil from a rifle—a rifle carefully taken care of."

"I still say—" Smythe said, but he looked around the room, and did not say at all. Sergeant Jones had put the rifle they were talking about down on the chair, and stood up, and was walking slowly down the room.

"I'm sorry, Mrs. Payne," Bill said. "I think it's now, don't you?"

"Now?" she said, and then breathed deeply and leaned back in the sofa again and looked across at Weigand, only at Weigand. "I wanted it to be a dream," she said. "You guessed that, didn't you? I—I prayed it would be a dream. Made myself—almost made myself—believe it was. You see—I had taken this stuff—everything was getting vague and—*it could have been a dream, couldn't it?*"

"Yes," Bill said. His voice was gentle.

"I wanted so much—" she said. "But, it's no good. I guess—I guess it's never going to be any good. I thought he—if he had—it was because—" She stopped again, for a moment closed her eyes, as if against pain. "It doesn't matter," she said. "In the end he tried to kill me, didn't he?"

"Yes."

"Last night," Lauren Payne said, "after I had gone to my room, I looked out the window. This must have been—oh, about half an hour before my husband was shot. Perhaps longer. I saw Blaine Smythe walk into the King Arthur Hotel. That's the hotel directly across the street. He was using crutches and he had a white bandage on his right foot." She stopped. Then, suddenly, her slender body began to shake with sobs. "I—" she said, and her voice shook, was almost inaudible. "I couldn't be the first to say it, could I? Did I—did I say it right? So that it's clear and everybody—"

Her head was back against the sofa's back. Her face was very white, and her body shook.

Blaine Smythe was standing—a tall, lithe man. He turned—started to turn—away. It was as if he meant to run.

Sergeant Jones put heavy hands, from behind, on Blaine Smythe's arms. "Wouldn't try anything if I were you," Jones said, and his voice was as heavy as his hands.

Gladys Mason was across the room, on the sofa beside Lauren Payne. She put an arm around Lauren's shaking body. She said, "There, child. There. It's over now."

16

The Siamese cat named Stilts lay on the carpet in front of the fire. She looked as if she had been scattered there. Shadow approached, enormous blue eyes all innocence. She sniffed Stilts briefly and bit her left hind foot.

With no preliminaries whatever, Stilts went three feet into the air, straight up. At the top, she turned, walked briefly on air, and came down on top of Shadow. Shadow flattened, and breath went out of her with a small sound like "uff." She turned on her back and began, furiously, to kick Stilts in the face. Stilts put both forelegs around Shadow's neck and began to bite her left ear.

"They do love each other," Pam North said, to anyone who cared to listen. "Don't you, babies?" she added, to the cats.

"It is," Dorian Weigand said, "impossible to jump like that. It is clearly impossible."

The sound of Dorian's voice distracted the cat named Shadow, who abandoned her obvious effort to kick Stilts to death and looked at Dorian. Stilts bit Shadow's tail. Shadow leaped three feet into the air, turned in flight, and came down on Stilts.

"All right," Dorian said. "Excuse it, please."

Dorian Weigand was curled, rather as a cat might herself curl, in a big chair in the Norths' apartment. It was a little after six on Thursday evening, and Dorian and the Norths had drinks and Bill was overdue for his.

"Here he comes now," Dorian said, uncurling. "Hear him?"

Pam and Jerry heard footsteps in the corridor outside. They sounded like any footsteps. But neither Pam nor Jerry really doubted; neither was surprised to hear a characteristic tapping on the door. Dorian let him in, looked at him carefully before kissing him. He didn't look any more tired than he usually did. He looked as if things had gone all right.

Things went well enough, he told them—told them after he had been supplied with a drink, and had swallowed half of it. Blaine Smythe was in the Fairfield County jail, charged with felonious assault, and with more to follow. He could fight extradition if he wanted to waste the time; if his lawyer thought it worth wasting. He denied everything and thereupon closed his lips, which was wise of him. But things went well enough.

A bell-man at the King Arthur, shown several photographs, had picked one of Smythe as resembling a man on crutches who had checked into the hotel late Tuesday afternoon, and been given—at request—a room on the third floor front. A cartridge case, ejected from the rifle which, in due time, would be described in newspapers as the murder weapon, had been found in grass behind a hedge. This had taken doing. From now on the things to be done would, for the most part, take doing. But they would get done. Things went well enough.

"Which," Bill said, and finished his drink and looked at an empty glass with absent-minded reproach, "gives us two of them. Thanks, Jerry."

"One in the grass we weren't to find, weren't even to look for," Bill said. "Another in the car—Self's car—which we were to find. A thorough man, Smythe. Thought of almost everything." He stopped, looked with absent-minded surprise at his replenished glass, sipped. "They've filled you in?" he said, to Dorian. "Up to now," Dorian said.

"Having gone to the trouble to get Self there," Bill said, "he didn't really leave any holes. A little put out, probably, to find you and the others there, Pam, but that needn't have been fatal. If, of course, his shot had been. Fired a shot from his rifle on the way up. It was his, incidentally. The other rifle was just—a prop. It was safe enough to fire. It's hunting season. He retrieved the casing and put it in his pocket. Reloaded, of course. After he knocked Self out, tossed the casing into the car."

"The trouble he went to," Pam said. "You jump around."

Bill looked at her in some surprise. He said he thought it obvious enough. When Smythe decided—it probably was decided reluctantly—that he had to kill Lauren, he decided also to provide the police with a murderer. A James Self, already complete enough with motive. So, he telephoned Self, pretending to be Lauren—

Bill interrupted himself. "She has a very deep,

216

rather husky voice," he said. "Symthe is an actor; Lars Simon says a good one. Good actors can mimic. Right?"

"Nobody's quarreling," Pam said. "Told Mr. Self Jo-An was there, got him to come, shot Mrs. Payne after Self arrived, rushed over and pretended to take the gun away from him while actually giving it to him. That's clear enough." She considered. "Now," she added.

"Right," Bill said. "Then it's all clear."

He seemed to consider the matter ended. He lighted a cigarette and leaned back; he blew smoke into the air and watched it.

"Don't tease the animals," Dorian told him. "Wouldn't it have been merely one word against another?"

"No," Bill said. "Lauren had called Smythe, asked him to come up. From the Dumont. There's a record of the call, complete with number. With her dead, he could quote her as he liked. Actually—I think still trying to think she had dreamed, still pushing reality away—she said—she can't remember her exact words—'I couldn't have seen you, could I? Not where I—I dreamed I did?' He reassured her, she says; almost convinced her. But—'He was too ready,' she said. 'I—I suppose then I really knew.'

"She must have revealed that—revealed she was not convinced. He made his decision then."

"Still—" Dorian said.

"At the time Self got the phone call," Bill said, "Lauren was in a garage in New Canaan, waiting for her car. She made no call from there. Nor was any long-distance call made from the house. So—a lie against Self. So—no explanation of his presence there. Except, of course, the one Smythe would provide. Along with the cartridge case in the car. Oh, I think it would have worked. With Mrs. Payne dead."

"You had this bandage gadget," Jerry pointed out. "With a streak on it. It was oil?"

"Yes. It was oil. I had that. Enough for a hunch. Not for proof. I'd have kept on worrying. Smythe wouldn't have needed to worry much."

"I don't," Dorian said, "see how he knew Mr. Payne would come out and stand on the sidewalk waiting to be shot at. If he hadn't, all this for nothing. Plus the chance somebody would see him—somebody who knew him—and want to commiserate about the broken leg or whatever."

"As for that," Bill said, "he could merely say he was getting the feel of the bandage gadget. Explain as much as necessary. He might, of course, have decided, under those circumstances, to postpone his sniping. The sniping, incidentally, because there's been a rash of them. And nobody caught. Another— well, say another tree in a woods."

"If you must," Dorian said, gently. "Now, darling—how he knew Mr. Payne would come out instead of having dinner at the hotel and going up to his room?"

Bill said, "Well—" He said, "I don't say everything's wrapped—"

"String," Pam said. "I save string, did you know? And wrapping paper. Payne thought the food at the Dumont was 'terrible.' They never ate there. Mrs. Payne told us that yesterday. Not you, Bill. He probably told everybody or—or she did. Of *course*. She and Blaine were—what were they, Bill? Anyway, she would have, wouldn't she?"

Bill thanked her for the string. He said it was a very

nice peice of string, a very useful piece of string. Or, if she preferred, wrapping.

"Bill," Pam said. "Why? Because they were lovers? He and Lauren? Even then, why?"

Bill emptied his glass. Jerry got up, and Bill put his hand over the glass. He said he would let the rest catch up.

"I don't think they were, Pam," he said, and spoke slowly. "She says not. She says that now she's glad—very glad. She says she doesn't know why they weren't. She said, 'I just couldn't bring myself—' and didn't finish. Not a matter of morals, I suspect. Of—" He shrugged. He said a psychiatrist might have a dozen reasons. He said that the word "revulsion" might sum it up. Revulsion instilled by other things; revulsion probably temporary.

"She talked a good deal about her husband," Bill said. "Nothing very—explicit. She's still—excited, upset. Not as coherent as she might be. I think because she's not very sure in her own mind. You see—she loved Smythe. Thought he loved her. But—about Payne. It seems he was something of a rat, as Self called him. In a—in a number of ways. What's called mental cruelty. She gets vague after that. But, I suspect it didn't stop there. That, somehow, he—well, left her in a kind of shock."

"Bill!" Pam said. "She's not up there all alone? Tearing herself to pieces alone?"

He looked surprised. He said he thought he had told her. Gladys Mason was with her. And the boy, too. "She seems," Bill said, "to have turned to Mrs. Mason. As to—oh, call it an elder sister."

"Hmmm," Dorian said. "As to the sister business." She sipped from her own drink.

"Call it what you like, then," Bill said. "Anyway,

219

she's turned to her. And Mrs. Mason is—protective."
He smiled faintly. "Shooed me out, in the end," he
said. "Seems to have taken over, in a very helpful
way. I've a feeling she may keep on with it."

"The ill wind," Pam said "But again—why? I realize I'm persistent."

"When she couldn't any longer believe in—in her
dream," Bill said. "She thought he had done it to
protect her. To—free her. Because he loved her."
Jerry made a gesture, started to speak. "No," Bill
said, "it's quite possible that that entered into it. At
one time, anyway. She—in a way she's defenseless. It
may even have started with that, only with that. She
still wants to believe that that was at the bottom of it."

"He tried to kill her," Jerry said. He went to the bar
and began to mix drinks. "And let's not quote Wilde,
please."

"Also," Bill said, "Payne got him fired. Quite un-
justly. Partly, at any rate, because that would hurt
Lauren. With Payne dead, he had his part back. Very
good part. Might have done a lot for him, Lars Simon
says. If the play had clicked."

"I like that better," Jerry said, and poured.

"Also," Bill said, "Mrs. Payne is quite a rich
woman. With Payne dead her—revulsion might well
have been overcome."

"I," Gerald North said, "like that best of all. And in
the end, of course, he was trying to save his own
neck."

He brought drinks on a tray.

"You're dour today," Pam said. "It's all those
things you have to read. Reaction."

"I'm dour," Jerry agreed. "You might have answered the door, Pam. You and Lauren are pretty
much of a size."

"Jerry!" Pam said, "it was her door."

He looked at her doubtfully. He started to refer to the sticking out of necks, but changed his mind. After all, nothing had happened to Pam's neck.

"As for the motive," Pam said. "It doesn't have to be just one, does it? It can be a scramble." She accepted a martini. "Things so often are," Pamela North said.